The Eyes of the World by Harold Bell Wright

Harold Bell Wright was born in Rome, New York on May 4th 1872. Wright had little to say that was good about his alcoholic father and his early years as he dragged "his wife and children from place to place, existing from hand to mouth, sinking deeper and deeper, as the years passed, into the slough of wretched poverty." His mother though introduced him to the great stories of literature and to appreciate the beauty of nature.

When Wright was 11, his mother died and his father abandoned them. Life was now time spent living with various relatives or strangers. He found odd jobs but frequently slept rough. In his late teens he found regular employment painting both pictures and houses but then turned to the Church. After two years at Hiram College in Hiram, Ohio, Wright became a minister for the Christian Church (Disciples of Christ) in Pierce City, Missouri and then pastored in Pittsburg, Kansas; Forest Avenue in Kansas City, Missouri; Lebanon, Missouri; and Redlands, California.

In 1902, while at the Church in Pittsburg, Kansas, he wrote a melodramatic story, 'That Printer of Udell's', to be read to his congregation. His church however serialised and published it in The Christian Century, their official journal. Wright despaired at the version printed but his parishioners encouraged him to write more. He took their advice. His second novel 'The Shepherd of the Hills' (1907) sold a million copies and established him as a best-selling author.

In 1909, pastors across America were incensed by his novel 'The Calling of Dan Matthews', which told a similar story to Wright's of a young preacher who resigns from the ministry in order to retain his integrity. They saw it as an attack on the Church but he that the Church was not doing its job properly. The book quickly sold a million copies.

Wright now resigned as pastor and dedicated his life to full time literature. In 1911, he published 'The Winning of Barbara Worth', a historical novel set in the Imperial Valley of southeastern California. Another million-seller.

With his next novel 'The Eyes of the World', Wright had the best-selling book of 1914 and another million-seller. He was a literary phenomenon and although today largely ignored he is one of the best-selling writers of all time.

From 1914 to about 1933 Wright lived mostly in Tucson, Arizona and then from 1935 until his death in 1944, he lived on his 'Quiet Hills Farm' near Escondido, California.

Between 1902 and 1942 Wright wrote 19 books, several stage plays, and a number of magazine articles.

For Wright though health was a major issue and increasingly so. He had struggled for most of his life with lung disease.

Harold Bell Wright died of bronchial pneumonia on May 24th, 1944 in Scripps Memorial Hospital in La Jolla, California.

"I have learned
To look on Nature not as in the hour

Of thoughtless youth; but hearing oftentimes
The sad, still music of humanity,
Not harsh or grating, though of ample power
To chasten and subdue. And I have felt,
A presence that disturbs me with the joy
Of elevated thoughts; a sense sublime
Of something far more deeply interfused,
Whose dwelling is in the lights of setting suns,
And the round ocean and the living air,
And the blue sky, and in the mind of man.
A motion and a spirit that impels
All thinking things, all objects of all thoughts,
And rolls through all things.

Therefore am I still
A lover of the meadows and the woods
And mountains.........
.... And this prayer I make,
Knowing that Nature never did betray
The heart that loved her. 'Tis her privilege
Through all the years of this one life, to lead
From joy to joy; for she can so inform
The mind that is within us—so impress
With quietness and beauty, and so feed
With lofty thoughts—that neither evil tongues,
Rash judgments, nor the sneers of selfish men,
Nor greetings where no kindness is, nor all
The dreary intercourse of daily life,
Shalt e'er prevail against us, or disturb
Our cheerful faith."

William Wordsworth.

Index of Contents

THE EYES OF THE WORLD

Chapter I

His Inheritance

It was winter—cold and snow and ice and naked trees and leaden clouds and stinging wind.

The house was an ancient mansion on an old street in that city of culture which has given to the history of our nation—to education, to religion, to the sciences, and to the arts—so many illustrious names.

In the changing years, before the beginning of my story, the woman's immediate friends and associates had moved from the neighborhood to the newer and more fashionable districts of a younger generation. In that city of her father's there were few of her old companions left. There were fewer who remembered. The distinguished leaders in the world of art and letters, whose voices had been so often heard within the walls of her home, had, one by one, passed on; leaving their works and their names to their children. The children, in the greedy rush of these younger times, had too readily forgotten the woman who, to the culture and genius of a passing day, had been hostess and friend.

The apartment was pitifully bare and empty. Ruthlessly it had been stripped of its treasures of art and its proud luxuries. But, even in its naked necessities the room managed, still, to evidence the rare intelligence and the exquisite refinement of its dying tenant.

The face upon the pillow, so wasted by sickness, was marked by the death-gray. The eyes, deep in their hollows between the fleshless forehead and the prominent cheek-bones, were closed; the lips were livid; the nose was sharp and pinched; the colorless cheeks were sunken; but the outlines were still delicately drawn and the proportions nobly fashioned. It was, still, the face of a gentlewoman. In the ashen lips, only, was there a sign of life; and they trembled and fluttered in their effort to utter the words that an indomitable spirit gave them to speak.

"To-day—to-day—he will—come." The voice was a thin, broken whisper; but colored, still, with pride and gladness.

A young woman in the uniform of a trained nurse turned quickly from the window. With soft, professional step, she crossed the room to bend over the bed. Her trained fingers sought the skeleton wrist; she spoke slowly, distinctly, with careful clearness; and, under the cool professionalism of her words, there was a tone of marked respect. "What is it, madam?"

The sunken eyes opened. As a burst of sunlight through the suddenly opened doors of a sepulchre, the death-gray face was illumed. In those eyes, clear and burning, the nurse saw all that remained of a powerful personality. In their shadowy depths, she saw the last glowing embers of the vital fire gathered; carefully nursed and tended; kept alive by a will that was clinging, with almost superhuman tenacity, to a definite purpose. Dying, this woman would not die—could not die—until the end for which she willed to live should be accomplished. In the very grasp of Death, she was forcing Death to stay his hand—without life, she was holding Death at bay.

It was magnificent, and the gentle face under the nurse's cap shone with appreciation and admiration as she smiled her sympathy and understanding.

"My son—my son—will come—to-day." The voice was stronger, and, with the eyes, expressed a conviction—a certainty—with the faintest shadow of a question.

The nurse looked at her watch. "The boat was due in New York, early this morning, madam."

A step sounded in the hall outside. The nurse started, and turned quickly toward the door. But the woman said, "The doctor." And, again, the fire that burned in those sunken eyes was hidden wearily under their dark lids.

The white-haired physician and the nurse, at the farther end of the room, spoke together in low tones. Said the physician,—incredulous,—"You say there is no change?"

"None that I can detect," breathed the nurse. "It is wonderful!"

"Her mind is clear?"

"As though she were in perfect health."

The doctor took the nurse's chart. For a moment, he studied it in silence. He gave it back with a gesture of amazement. "God! nurse," he whispered, "she should be in her grave by now! It's a miracle! But she has always been like that—" he continued, half to himself, looking with troubled admiration toward the bed at the other end of the room—"always."

He went slowly forward to the chair that the nurse placed for him. Seating himself quietly beside his patient, and bending forward with intense interest, his fine old head bowed, he regarded with more than professional care the wasted face upon the pillow.

The doctor remembered, too well, when those finely moulded features—now, so worn by sorrow, so marked by sickness, so ghastly in the hue of death—were rounded with young-woman health and tinted with rare loveliness. He recalled that day when he saw her a bride. He remembered the sweet, proud dignity of her young wifehood. He saw her, again, when her face shone with the glad triumph and the holy joy of motherhood.

The old physician turned from his patient, to look with sorrowful eyes about the room that was to witness the end.

Why was such a woman dying like this? Why was a life of such rich mental and spiritual endowments— of such wealth of true culture—coming to its close in such material poverty?

The doctor was one of the few who knew. He was one of the few who understood that, to the woman herself, it was necessary.

There were those who—without understanding, for the sake of the years that were gone—would have surrounded her with the material comforts to which, in her younger days, she had been accustomed. The doctor knew that there was one—a friend of her childhood, famous, now, in the world of books— who would have come from the ends of the earth to care for her. All that a human being could do for her, in those days of her life's tragedy, that one had done. Then—because he understood—he had gone away. Her own son did not know—could not, in his young manhood, have understood, if he had known—would not understand when he came. Perhaps, some day, he would understand—perhaps.

When the physician turned again toward the bed, to touch with gentle fingers the wrist of his patient, his eyes were wet.

At his touch, her eyes opened to regard him with affectionate trust and gratitude.

"Well Mary," he said almost bruskly.

The lips fashioned the ghost of a smile; into her eyes came the gleam of that old time challenging spirit. "Well—Doctor George," she answered. Then,—"I—told you—I would not—go—until he came. I must— have my way—still—you see. He will—come—to-day He must come."

"Yes, Mary," returned the doctor,—his fingers still on the thin wrist, and his eyes studying her face with professional keenness,—"yes, of course."

"And George—you will not forget—your promise? You will—give me a few minutes—of strength—when he comes—so that I can tell him? I—I—must tell him myself—George. You—will do—this last thing—for me?"

"Yes, Mary, of course," he answered again. "Everything shall be as you wish—as I promised."

"Thank you—George. Thank you—my dear—dear—old friend."

The nurse—who had been standing at the window—stepped quickly to the table that held a few bottles, glasses, and instruments. The doctor looked at her sharply. She nodded a silent answer, as she opened a small, flat, leather case. With his fingers still on his patient's wrist, the physician spoke a word of instruction; and, in a moment, the nurse placed a hypodermic needle in his hand.

As the doctor gave the instrument, again, to his assistant, a quick step sounded in the hall outside.

The patient turned her head. Her eager eyes were fixed upon the door; her voice—stronger, now, with the strength of the powerful stimulant—rang out; "My boy—my boy—he is here! George, nurse, my boy is here!"

The door opened. A young man of perhaps twenty-two years stood on the threshold.

The most casual observer would have seen that he was a son of the dying woman. In the full flush of his young manhood's vigor, there was the same modeling of the mouth, the same nose with finely turned nostrils, the same dark eyes under a breadth of forehead; while the determined chin and the well-squared jaw, together with a rather remarkable fineness of line, told of an inherited mental and spiritual strength and grace as charming as it is, in these days, rare. His dress was that of a gentleman of culture and social position. His very bearing evidenced that he had never been without means to gratify the legitimate tastes of a cultivated and refined intelligence.

As he paused an instant in the open door to glance about that poverty stricken room, a look of bewildering amazement swept over his handsome face. He started to draw back—as if he had unintentionally entered the wrong apartment. Looking at the doctor, his lips parted as if to apologize for his intrusion. But before he could speak, his eyes met the eyes of the woman on the bed.

With a cry of horror, he sprang forward;—"Mother! Mother!"

As he knelt there by the bed, when the first moments of their meeting were past, he turned his face toward the doctor. From the physician his gaze went to the nurse, then back again to his mother's old friend. His eyes were burning with shame and sorrow—with pain and doubt and accusation. His low voice was tense with emotion, as he demanded, "What does this mean? Why is my mother here like—like this?"—his eyes swept the bare room again.

The dying woman answered. "I will explain, my boy. It is to tell you, that I have waited."

At a look from the doctor, the nurse quietly followed the physician from the room.

It was not long. When she had finished, the false strength that had kept the woman alive until she had accomplished that which she conceived to be her last duty, failed quickly.

"You will—promise—you will?"

"Yes, mother, yes."

"Your education—your training—your blood—they—are—all—that—I can—give you, my son."

"O mother, mother! why did you not tell me before? Why did I not know!" The cry was a protest—an expression of bitterest shame and sorrow.

She smiled. "It—was—all that I could do—for you—my son—the only way—I could—help. I do not—regret the cost. You will—not forget?"

"Never, mother, never."

"You promise—to—to regain that—which—your father—"

Solemnly the answer came,—in an agony of devotion and love,—"I promise—yes, mother, I promise."

A month later, the young man was traveling, as fast as modern steam and steel could carry him, toward the western edge of the continent.

He was flying from the city of his birth, as from a place accursed. He had set his face toward a new land—determined to work out, there, his promise—the promise that he did not, at the first, understand.

How he misunderstood,—how he attempted to use his inheritance to carry out what he first thought was his mother's wish,—and how he came at last to understand, is the story that I have to tell.

Chapter II

The Woman with the Disfigured Face

The Golden State Limited, with two laboring engines, was climbing the desert side of San Gorgonio Pass.

Now San Gorgonio Pass—as all men should know—is one of the two eastern gateways to the beautiful heart of Southern California. It is, therefore, the gateway to the scenes of my story.

As the heavy train zigzagged up the long, barren slope of the mountain, in its effort to lessen the heavy grade, the young man on the platform of the observation car could see, far to the east, the shimmering, sun-filled haze that lies, always, like a veil of mystery, over the vast reaches of the Colorado Desert. Now and then, as the Express swung around the curves, he gained a view of the lonely, snow-piled peaks of the San Bernardinos; with old San Gorgonio, lifting above the pine-fringed ridges of the lower Galenas, shining, silvery white, against the blue. Again, on the southern side of the pass, he saw San Jacinto's crags and cliffs rising almost sheer from the right-of-way.

But the man watching the ever-changing panorama of gorgeously colored and fantastically unreal landscape was not thinking of the scenes that, to him, were new and strange. His thoughts were far away. Among those mountains grouped about San Gorgonio, the real value of the inheritance he had received from his mother was to be tested. On the pine-fringed ridge of the Galenas, among those granite cliffs and jagged peaks, the mettle of his manhood was to be tried under a strain such as few men in this commonplace work-a-day old world are-subjected to. But the young man did not know this.

On the long journey across the continent, he had paid little heed to the sights that so interested his fellow passengers. To his fellow passengers, themselves, he had been as indifferent. To those who had approached him casually, as the sometimes tedious hours passed, he had been quietly and courteously unresponsive. This well-bred but decidedly marked disinclination to mingle with them, together with the undeniably distinguished appearance of the young man, only served to center the interest of the little world of the Pullmans more strongly upon him. Keeping to himself, and engrossed with his own thoughts, he became the object of many idle conjectures.

Among the passengers whose curious eyes were so often turned in his direction, there was one whose interest was always carefully veiled. She was a woman of evident rank and distinction in that world where rank and distinction are determined wholly by dollars and by such social position as dollars can buy. She was beautiful; but with that carefully studied, wholly self-conscious—one is tempted to say professional—beauty of her kind. Her full rounded, splendidly developed body was gowned to accentuate the alluring curves of her sex. With such skill was this deliberate appeal to the physical hidden under a cloak of a pretending modesty that its charm was the more effectively revealed. Her features were almost too perfect. She was too coldly sure of herself—too perfectly trained in the art of self-repression. For a woman as young as she evidently was, she seemed to know too much. The careful indifference of her countenance seemed to say, "I am too well schooled in life to make mistakes." She was traveling with two companions—a fluffy, fluttering, characterless shadow of womanhood, and a man—an invalid who seldom left the privacy of the drawing-room which he occupied.

As the train neared the summit of the pass, the young man on the observation car platform looked at his watch. A few miles more and he would arrive at his destination. Rising to his feet, he drew a deep breath of the glorious, sun-filled air. With his back to the door, and looking away into the distance, he did not notice the woman who, stepping from the car at that moment, stood directly behind him, steadying herself by the brass railing in front of the window. To their idly observing fellow passengers, the woman, too, appeared interested in the distant landscape. She might have been looking at the only other occupant of the platform. The passengers, from where they sat, could not have told.

As he stood there,—against the background of the primitive, many-colored landscape,—the young man might easily have attracted the attention of any one. He would have attracted attention in a crowd. Tall, with an athletic trimness of limb, a good breadth of shoulder, and a fine head poised with that natural, unconscious pride of the well-bred—he kept his feet on the unsteady platform of the car with that easy grace which marks only well-conditioned muscles, and is rarely seen save in those whose lives are sanely clean.

The Express had entered the yards at the summit station, and was gradually lessening its speed. Just as the man turned to enter the car, the train came to a full stop, and the sudden jar threw him almost into the arms of the woman. For an instant, while he was struggling to regain his balance, he was so close to her that their garments touched. Indeed, he only prevented an actual collision by throwing his arm across her shoulder and catching the side of the car window against which she was leaning.

In that moment, while his face was so close to hers that she might have felt his breath upon her cheek and he was involuntarily looking straight into her eyes, the man felt, queerly, that the woman was not shrinking from him. In fact, one less occupied with other thoughts might have construed her bold, open look, her slightly parted lips and flushed cheeks, as a welcome—quite as though she were in the habit of having handsome young men throw themselves into her arms.

Then, with a hint of a smile in his eyes, he was saying, conventionally, "I beg your pardon. It was very stupid of me."

As he spoke, a mask of cold indifference slipped over her face. Without deigning to notice his courteous apology, she looked away, and, moving to the railing of the platform, became ostensibly interested in the busy activity of the railroad yards.

Had the woman—in that instant when his arm was over her shoulder and his eyes were looking into hers—smiled, the incident would have slipped quickly from his mind. As it was, the flash-like impression of the moment remained, and—

Down the steep grade of the narrow San Timateo Canyon, on the coast side of the mountain pass, the Overland thundered on the last stretch of its long race to the western edge of the continent. And now, from the car windows, the passengers caught tantalizing glimpses of bright pastures with their herds of contented dairy cows, and with their white ranch buildings set in the shade of giant pepper and eucalyptus trees. On the rounded shoulders and steep flanks of the foothills that form the sides of the canyon, the barley fields looked down upon the meadows; and, now and then, in the whirling landscape winding side canyons—beautiful with live-oak and laurel, with greasewood and sage—led the eye away toward the pine-fringed ridges of the Galenas while above, the higher snow-clad peaks and domes of the San Bernardinos still shone coldly against the blue.

In the Pullman, there was a stir of awakening interest The travel-wearied passengers, laying aside books and magazines and cards, renewed conversations that, in the last monotonous hours of the desert part of the journey, had lagged painfully. Throughout the train, there was an air of eager expectancy; a bustling movement of preparation. The woman of the observation car platform had disappeared into her stateroom. The young man gathered his things together in readiness to leave the train at the next stop.

In the flying pictures framed by the windows, the dairy pastures and meadows were being replaced by small vineyards and orchards; the canyon wall, on the northern side, became higher and steeper, shutting out the mountains in the distance and showing only a fringe of trees on the sharp rim; while against the gray and yellow and brown and green of the chaparral on the steep, untilled bluffs, shone the silvery softness of the olive trees that border the arroyo at their feet.

With a long, triumphant shriek, the flying overland train—from the lands of ice and snow—from barren deserts and lonely mountains—rushed from the narrow mouth of the canyon, and swept out into the beautiful San Bernardino Valley where the travelers were greeted by wide, green miles of orange and lemon and walnut and olive groves—by many acres of gardens and vineyards and orchards. Amid these groves and gardens, the towns and cities are set; their streets and buildings half hidden in wildernesses of eucalyptus and peppers and palms; while—towering above the loveliness of the valley and visible now from the sweeping lines of their foothills to the gleaming white of their lonely peaks—rises, in blue-veiled, cloud-flecked steeps and purple shaded canyons, the beauty and grandeur of the mountains.

It was January. To those who had so recently left the winter lands, the Southern California scene—so richly colored with its many shades of living green, so warm in its golden sunlight—seemed a dream of fairyland. It was as though that break in the mountain wall had ushered them suddenly into another world—a world, strange, indeed, to eyes accustomed to snow and ice and naked trees and leaden clouds.

Among the many little cities half concealed in the luxurious, semi-tropical verdure of the wide valley at the foot of the mountains, Fairlands—if you ask a citizen of that well-known mecca of the tourist—is easily the Queen. As for that! all our Southern California cities are set in wildernesses of beauty; all are in wide valleys; all are at the foot of the mountains; all are meccas for tourists; each one—if you ask a citizen—is the Queen. If you, perchance should question this fact—write for our advertising literature.

Passengers on the Golden State Limited—as perhaps you know—do not go direct to Fairlands. They change at Fairlands Junction. The little city, itself, is set in the lap of the hills that form the southern side of the valley, some three miles from the main line. It is as though this particular "Queen" withdrew from the great highway traveled by the vulgar herd—in the proud aloofness of her superior clay, sufficient unto herself. The soil out of which Fairlands is made is much richer, it is said, than the common dirt of her sister cities less than fifteen miles distant. A difference of only a few feet in elevation seems, strangely, to give her a much more rarefied air. Her proudest boast is that she has a larger number of millionaires in proportion to her population than any other city in the land.

It was these peculiar and well-known advantages of Fairlands that led the young man of my story to select it as the starting point of his worthy ambition. And Fairlands is a good place for one so richly endowed with an inheritance that cannot be expressed in dollars to try his strength. Given such a community, amid such surroundings, with a man like the young man of my story, and something may be depended upon to happen.

While the travelers from the East, bound for Fairlands, were waiting at the Junction for the local train that would take them through the orange groves to their journey's end, the young man noticed the woman of the observation car platform with her two companions. And now, as he paced to and fro, enjoying the exercise after the days of confinement in the Pullman, he observed them with stimulated interest—they, too, were going to Fairlands.

The man of the party, though certainly not old in years, was frightfully aged by dissipation and disease. The gross, sensual mouth with its loose-hanging lips; the blotched and clammy skin; the pale, watery eyes with their inflamed rims and flabby pouches; the sunken chest, skinny neck and limbs; and the thin rasping voice—all cried aloud the shame of a misspent life. It was as clearly evident that he was a man of wealth and, in the eyes of the world, of an enviable social rank.

As the young man passed and repassed them, where they stood under the big pepper tree that shades the depot, the man—in his harsh, throaty whisper, between spasms of coughing—was cursing the train service, the country, the weather; and, apparently, whatever else he could think of as being worthy or unworthy his impotent ill-temper. The shadowy suggestion of womanhood—glancing toward the young man—was saying, with affected giggles, "O papa, don't! Oh isn't it perfectly lovely! O papa, don't! Do hush! What will people think?" This last variation of his daughter's plaint must have given the man some satisfaction, at least, for it furnished him another target for his pointless shafts; and he fairly outdid himself in politely damning whoever might presume to think anything at all of him; with the net result that two Mexicans, who were loafing near enough to hear, grinned with admiring amusement. The woman stood a little apart from the others. Coldly indifferent alike to the man's cursing and coughing and to the daughter's ejaculations, she appeared to be looking at the mountains. But the young man fancied that, once or twice, as he faced about at the end of his beat, her eyes were turned in his direction.

When the Fairlands train came in, the three found seats conveniently turned, near the forward end of the car. The young man, in passing, glanced down; and the woman, who had taken the chair next to the aisle, looked up full into his face.

Again, as their eyes met, the man felt—as when they had stood so close together on the platform of the observation car—that she did not shrink from him. It was only for an instant. Then, glancing about for a seat, he saw another face—a face, in its outlines, so like the one into which he had just looked, and yet so different—so far removed in its expression and meaning—that it fixed his attention instantly— compelling his interest.

As this woman sat looking from the car window away toward the distant mountain peaks, the young man thought he had never seen a more perfect profile; nor a countenance that expressed such a beautiful blending of wistful longing, of patient fortitude, and saintly resignation. It was the face of a Madonna,—but a Madonna after the crucifixion,—pathetic in its lonely sorrow, inspiring in its spiritual strength, and holy in its purity and freedom from earthly passions.

She was near his mother's age; and looking at her—as he moved down the aisle—his mother's face, as he had known it before their last meeting, came to him with startling vividness. For an instant, he paused, moved to take the chair beside her; but the next two seats were vacant, and he had no excuse for intruding. Arranging his grips, he quickly seated himself next to the window; and again, with eager interest, turned toward the woman in the chair ahead. Involuntarily, he started with astonishment and pity.

The woman—still gazing from the window at the distant mountain peaks, and seemingly unconscious of her surroundings—presented now, to the man's shocked and compassionate gaze, the other side of her face. It was hideously disfigured by a great scar that—covering the entire cheek and neck—distorted the corner of the mouth, drew down the lower lid of the eye, and twisted her features into an ugly caricature. Even the ear, half hidden under the soft, gray-threaded hair, had not escaped, but was deformed by the same dreadful agent that had wrought such ruin to one of the loveliest countenances the man had ever looked upon.

When the train stopped at Fairlands, and the passengers crowded into the aisle to make their way out, of the characters belonging to my story, the woman with the man and his daughter went first. Following them, a half car-length of people between, went the woman with the disfigured face.

On the depot platform, as they moved toward the street, the young man still held his place near the woman who had so awakened his pitying interest. The three Overland passengers were met by a heavy-faced thick-necked man who escorted them to a luxurious touring car.

The invalid and his daughter had entered the automobile when their escort, in turning toward the other member of the party, saw the woman with the disfigured face—who was now quite near. Instantly, he paused. And there was a smile of recognition on his somewhat coarse features as, lifting his hat, he bowed with—the young man fancied—condescending politeness. The woman standing by his side with her hand upon the door of the automobile, seeing her companion saluting some one, turned—and the next moment, the two women, whose features seemed so like—yet so unlike—were face to face.

The young man saw the woman with the disfigured face stop short. For an instant, she stood as though dazed by an unexpected blow. Then, holding out her hands with a half-pleading, half-groping gesture, she staggered and would have fallen had he not stepped to her side.

"Permit me, madam; you are ill."

She neither spoke nor moved; but, with her eyes fixed upon the woman by the automobile, allowed him to support her—seemingly unconscious of his presence. And never before had the young man seen such anguish of spirit written in a human countenance.

The one who had saluted her, advanced—as though to offer his services. But, as he moved toward her, she shrank back with a low—"No, no!" And such a look of horror and fear came into her eyes that the man by her side felt his muscles tense with indignation.

Looking straight into the heavy face of the stranger, he said curtly, "I think you had better go on."

With a careless shrug, the other turned and went back to the automobile, where he spoke in a low tone to his companions.

The woman, who had been watching with a cold indifference, stepped into the car. The man took his seat by the chauffeur. As the big machine moved away, the woman with the disfigured face, again made as if to stretch forth her hands in a pleading gesture.

The young man spoke pityingly; "May I assist you to a carriage, madam?"

At his words, she looked up at him and—seeming to find in his face the strength she needed—answered in a low voice, "Thank you, sir; I am better now. I will he all right, presently, if you will put me on the car." She indicated a street-car that was just stopping at the crossing.

"Are you quite sure that you are strong enough?" he asked kindly, as he walked with her toward the car.

"Yes,"—with a sad attempt to smile,—"yes, and I thank you very much, sir, for your gentle courtesy."

He assisted her up the step of the car, and stood with bared head as she passed inside, and the conductor gave the signal.

The incident had attracted little attention from the passengers who were hurrying from the train. Their minds were too intent upon other things to more than glance at this little ripple on the surface of life. Those who had chanced to notice the woman's agitation had seen, also, that she was being cared for; and so had passed on, giving the scene no second thought.

When the man returned from the street to his grips on the depot platform, the hacks and hotel buses were gone. As he stood looking about, questioningly, for some one who might direct him to a hotel, his eyes fell upon a strange individual who was regarding him intently.

Fully six feet in height, the observer was so lean that he suggested the unpleasant appearance of a living skeleton. His narrow shoulders were so rounded, his form was so stooped, that the young man's first thought was to wonder how tall he would really be if he could stand erect. His long, thin face, seamed and lined, was striking in its grotesque ugliness. From under his craggy, scowling brows, his sharp green-gray eyes peered with a curious expression of baffling, quizzing, half pathetic, and wholly cynical, interrogation. He was smoking a straight, much-used brier pipe. At his feet, lay a beautiful Irish Setter dog.

Half hidden by a supporting column of the depot portico—as if to escape the notice of the people in the automobile—he had been watching the woman with the disfigured face, with more than casual interest. He turned, now, upon the young man who had so kindly given her assistance.

In answer to the stranger's inquiry, with a curt sentence and a nod of his head he directed him to a hotel—two blocks away.

Thanking him, the young man, carrying his grips, set out. Upon reaching the street, he involuntarily turned to look back.

The oddly appearing character had not moved from his place, but stood, still looking after the stranger—the brier pipe in his mouth, the Irish Setter at his feet.

Chapter III

The Famous Conrad Lagrange

When the young man reached the hotel, he went at once to his room, where he passed the time between the hour of his arrival and the evening meal.

Upon his return to the lobby, the first object that attracted his eyes was the uncouth figure of the man whom he had seen at the depot, and who had directed him to the hotel.

That oddly appearing individual, his brier pipe still in his mouth and the Irish Setter at his feet, was standing—or rather lounging—at the clerk's counter, bending over the register; an attitude which—making his skeleton-like form more round shouldered than ever—caused him to present the general outlines of a rude interrogation point.

In the dining-room, a few minutes later, the two men sat at adjoining tables; and the young man heard his neighbor bullying the waiters and commenting in an audible undertone, upon every dish that was served to him—swearing by all the heathen gods, known and unknown, that there was nothing fit to eat in the house; and that if it were not for the fact that there was no place else in the cursed town that served half so good, he would not touch a mouthful in the place. Then, to the other's secret amusement he fell to right heartily and made an astonishing meal of the really excellent viands he had so roundly vilified.

Dinner over, the young man went with his cigar to the long veranda; intent upon enjoying the restful quiet of the evening after the tiresome days on the train. Carrying a chair to an unoccupied corner, he had his cigar just nicely under way when the Irish Setter—with all the dignity of his royal blood—approached. Resting a seal-brown head, with its long silky ears, confidently upon the stranger's knee, the dog looked up into the man's face with an expression of hearty good-fellowship in his soft, golden-brown eyes that was irresistible.

"Good dog," said the man, heartily, "good old fellow," and stroked the sleek head and neck, affectionately.

A whiff of pipe smoke drifted over his shoulder, and he looked around. The dog's master stood just behind him; regarding him with that quizzing, half pathetic, half humorous, and altogether cynical expression.

The young man who had been so unresponsive to the advances of his fellow passengers, for some reason—unknown, probably, to himself—now took the initiative. "You have a fine dog here, sir," he said encouragingly.

Without replying, the other turned away and in another moment returned with a chair; whereupon the dog, with slightly waving, feathery tail, transferred his attention to his master.

Caressing the seal-brown head with a gentle hand, and apparently speaking to the soft eyes that looked up at him so understandingly, the man said, "If the human race was fit to associate with such dogs, the world would be a more comfortable place to live in." The deep voice that rumbled up from some unguessed depths of that sunken chest was remarkable in its suggestion of a virile power that the general appearance of the man seemed to deny. Facing his companion suddenly, he asked with a direct bluntness, "Are you not Aaron King—son of the Aaron King of New England political fame?"

Under the searching gaze of those green-gray eyes, the young man flushed. "Yes; my father was active in New England politics," he answered simply. "Did you know him?"

"Very well"—returned the other—"very well." He repeated the two words with a suggestive emphasis; his eyes—with that curious, baffling, questioning look—still fixed upon his companion's face.

The red in Aaron King's cheeks deepened.

Looking away, the strange man added, with a softer note in his rough voice, "I thought I knew you, when I saw you at the depot. Your mother and I were boy and girl together. There is a little of her face in yours. If you have as much of her character, you are to be congratulated—and—so are the rest of us." The last words were spoken, apparently, to the dog; who, still looking up at him, seemed to express with slow-waving tail, an understanding of thoughts that were only partly put into words.

There was an impersonality in the man's personalities that made it impossible for the subject of his observations to take offense.

Aaron King—when it was evident that the man had no thought of introducing himself—said, with the fine courtesy that seemed always to find expression in his voice and manner, "May I ask your name, sir?"

The other, without turning his eyes from the dog, answered, "Conrad Lagrange."

The young man smiled. "I am very pleased to meet you, Mr. Lagrange. Surely, you are not the famous novelist of that name?"

"And why, 'surely not'?" retorted the other, again turning his face quickly toward his companion. "Am I not distinguished enough in appearance? Do I look like the mob? True, I am a scrawny, humpbacked crooked-faced, scarecrow of a man—but what matters that, if I do not look like the mob? What is called fame is as scrawny and humpbacked and crooked-faced as my body—but what matters that? Famous or infamous—to not look like the mob is the thing."

It is impossible to put in print the peculiar humor of pathetic regret, of sarcasm born of contempt, of intolerant intellectual pride, that marked the last sentence, which was addressed to the dog, as though the speaker turned from his human companion to a more worthy listener.

When Aaron King could find no words to reply, the novelist shot another question at him, with startling suddenness. "Do you read my books?"

The other began a halting answer to the effect that everybody read Conrad Lagrange's books. But the distinguished author interrupted; "Don't take the trouble to lie—out of politeness. I shall ask you to tell me about them and you will be in a hole."

The young man laughed as he said, with straight-forward frankness, "I have read only one, Mr. Lagrange."

"Which one?"

"The—ah—why—the one, you know—where the husband of one woman falls in love with the wife of another who is in love with the husband of some one else. Pshaw!—what is the title? I mean the one that created such a furore, you know."

"Yes"—said the man, to his dog—"O yes, Czar—I am the famous Conrad Lagrange. I observe"—he added, turning to the other, with twinkling eyes—"I observe, Mr. King, that you really do have a good bit of your mother's character. That you do not read my books is a recommendation that I, better than any one, know how to appreciate." The light of humor went from his face, suddenly, as it had come. Again he turned away; and his deep voice was gentle as he continued, "Your mother is a rare and beautiful spirit, sir. Knowing her regard for the true and genuine,—her love for the pure and beautiful,—I scarcely expected to find her son interested in the realism of my fiction. I congratulate you, young man"—he paused; then added with indescribable bitterness—"that you have not read my books."

For a few moments, Aaron King did not answer. At last, with quiet dignity, he said, "My mother was a remarkable woman, Mr. Lagrange."

The other faced him quickly. "You say was? Do you mean—?"

"My mother is dead, sir. I was called home from abroad by her illness."

For a little, the older man sat looking into the gathering dusk. Then, deliberately, he refilled his brier pipe, and, rising, said to his dog, "Come, Czar—it's time to go."

Without a word of parting to his human companion with the dog moving sedately by his side, he disappeared into the darkness of the night.

All the next day, Aaron King—in the hotel dining-room, the lobby, and on the veranda—watched for the famous novelist. Even on the streets of the little city, he found himself hoping to catch a glimpse of the uncouth figure and the homely, world-worn face of the man whose unusual personality had so attracted him. The day was nearly gone when Conrad Lagrange again appeared. As on the evening before, the young man was smoking his after-dinner cigar on the veranda, when the Irish Setter and a whiff of pipe smoke announced the strange character's presence.

Without taking a seat, the novelist said, "I always have a look at the mountains, at this time of the day, Mr. King—would you care to come? These mountains are the real thing, you know, and well worth seeing—particularly at this hour." There was a gentle softness in his deep voice, now—as unlike his usual speech as his physical appearance was unlike that of his younger companion.

Aaron King arose quickly. "Thank you, Mr, Lagrange; I will go with pleasure."

Accompanied by the dog, they followed the avenue, under the giant pepper trees that shut out the sky with their gnarled limbs and gracefully drooping branches, to the edge of the little city; where the view to the north and northeast was unobstructed by houses. Just where the street became a road, Conrad Lagrange—putting his hand upon his companion's arm—said in a low voice, "This is the place."

Behind them, beautiful Fairlands lay, half lost, in its wilderness of trees and flowers. Immediately in the foreground, a large tract of unimproved land brought the wild grasses and plants to their very feet. Beyond these acres—upon which there were no trees—the orange groves were massed in dark green blocks and squares; with, here and there, thin rows of palms; clumps of peppers; or tall, plume-like eucalyptus; to mark the roads and the ranch homes. Beyond this—and rising, seemingly, out of the groves—the San Bernardinos heaved their mighty masses into the sky. It was almost dark. The city's lamps were lighted. The outlines of grove and garden were fast being lost in the deepening dusk. The foothills, with the lower spurs and ridges of the mountains, were softly modeled in dark blue against the deeper purple of the canyons and gorges. Upon the cloudless sky that was lighted with clearest saffron, the lines of the higher crests were sharply drawn; while the lonely, snow-capped peaks,—ten thousand feet above the darkening valley below,—catching the last rays of the sun, glowed rose-pink—changing to salmon—deepening into mauve—as the light failed.

Aaron King broke the silence by drawing a long breath—as one who could find no words to express his emotions.

Conrad Lagrange spoke sadly; "And to think that there are,—in this city of ten thousand,—probably, nine thousand nine hundred and ninety people who never see it."

With a short laugh, the young man said, "It makes my fingers fairly itch for my palette and brushes—though it's not at all my sort of thing."

The other turned toward him quickly. "You are an artist?"

"I had just completed my three years study abroad when mother's illness brought me home. I was fortunate enough to get one on the line, and they say—over there—that I had a good chance. I don't know how it will go here at home." There was a note of anxiety in his voice.

"What do you do?"

"Portraits."

[Illustration: A curious expression of baffling quizzing half pathetic and wholly cynical interrogation]

With his face again toward the mountains, the novelist said thoughtfully, "This West country will produce some mighty artists, Mr. King. By far the greater part of this land must remain, always, in its primitive naturalness. It will always be easier, here, than in the city crowded East, for a man to be himself. There is less of that spirit which is born of clubs and cliques and clans and schools—with their fine-spun theorizing, and their impudent assumption that they are divinely commissioned to sit in judgment. There is less of artistic tea-drinking, esthetic posing, and soulful talk; and more opportunity for that loneliness out of which great art comes. The atmosphere of these mountains and deserts and seas inspires to a self-assertion, rather than to a clinging fast to the traditions and culture of others—and what, after all, is a great artist, but one who greatly asserts himself?"

The younger man answered in a like vein; "Mr. Lagrange, your words recall to my mind a thought in one of mother's favorite books. She quoted from the volume so often that, as a youngster, I almost knew it by heart, and, in turn, it became my favorite. Indeed, I think that, with mother's aid as an interpreter, it has had more influence upon my life than any other one book. This is the thought: 'To understand the message of the mountains; to love them for what they are; and, in terms of every-day life, to give expression to that understanding and love—is a mark of true greatness of soul.' I do not know the author. The book is anonymous."

"I am the author of that book, sir," the strange man answered with simple dignity, "—or, rather,—I should say,—I was the author," he added, with a burst of his bitter, sarcastic humor. "For God's sake don't betray me. I am, now, the famous Conrad Lagrange, you understand. I have a name to protect." His deep voice was shaken with feeling. His worn and rugged features twitched and worked with emotion.

Aaron King listened in amazement to the words that were spoken by the famous novelist with such pathetic regret and stinging self-accusation. Not knowing how to reply, he said casually, "You are working here, Mr. Lagrange?"

"Working! Me? I don't work anywhere. I am a literary scavenger. I haunt the intellectual slaughter pens, and live by the putrid offal that self-respecting writers reject. I glean the stinking materials for my stories from the sewers and cesspools of life. For the dollars they pay, I furnish my readers with those thrills that public decency forbids them to experience at first hand. I am a procurer for the purposes of mental prostitution. My books breed moral pestilence and spiritual disease. The unholy filth I write fouls the minds and pollutes the imaginations of my readers. I am an instigator of degrading immorality and unmentionable crimes. Work! No, young man, I don't work. Just now, I'm doing penance in this damned town. My rotten imaginings have proven too much—even for me—and the doctors sent me West to recuperate,"

The artist could find no words that would answer. In silence, the two men turned away from the mountains, and started back along the avenue by which they had come.

When they had walked some little distance, the young man said, "This is your first visit to Fairlands, Mr. Lagrange?"

"I was here last year"—answered the other—"here and in the hills yonder. Have you been much in the mountains?"

"Not in California. This is my first trip to the West. I have seen something of the mountains, though, at tourist resorts—abroad."

"Which means," commented the other, "that you have never seen them at all."

Aaron King laughed. "I dare say you are right."

"And you—?" asked the novelist, abruptly, eyeing his companion. "What brought you to this community that thinks so much more of its millionaires than it does of its mountains? Have you come to Fairlands to work?"

"I hope to," answered the artist. "There are—there are reasons why I do not care to work, for the present, in the East. I confess it was because I understood that Fairlands offered exceptional opportunities for a portrait painter that I came here. To succeed in my work, you know, one must come in touch with people of influence. It is sometimes easier to interest them when they are away from their homes—in some place like this—where their social duties and business cares are not so pressing."

"There is no question of the material that Fairlands has to offer, Mr. King," returned the novelist, in his grim, sarcastic humor. "God! how I envy you!" he added, with a flash of earnest passion. "You are young—You are beginning your life work—You are looking forward to success—You—"

"I must succeed"—the painter interrupted impetuously—"I must."

"Succeed in what? What do you mean by success?"

"Surely, you should understand what I mean by success," the younger man retorted. "You who have gained—"

"Oh, yes; I forgot"—came the quick interruption—"I am the famous Conrad Lagrange. Of course, you, too, must succeed. You must become the famous Aaron King. But perhaps you will tell me why you must, as you call it, succeed?"

The artist hesitated before answering; then said with anxious earnestness, "I don't think I can explain Mr. Lagrange. My mother—" he paused.

The older man stopped short, and, turning, stood for a little with his face towards the mountains where San Bernardino's pyramid-like peak was thrust among the stars. When he spoke, every bit of that bitter humor was gone from his deep voice. "I beg your pardon, Mr. King"—he said slowly—"I am as ugly and misshapen in spirit as in body."

But when they had walked some way—again in silence—and were drawing near the hotel, the momentary change in his mood passed. In a tone of stinging sarcasm he said. "You are on the right road, Mr. King. You did well to come to Fairlands. It is quite evident that you have mastered the modern technic of your art. To acquire fame, you have only to paint pictures of fast women who have no morals at all—making them appear as innocent maidens, because they have the price to pay, and, in the eyes of the world, are of social importance. Put upon your canvases what the world will call portraits of distinguished citizens—making low-browed money—thugs to look like noble patriots, and bloody butchers of humanity like benevolent saints. You need give yourself no uneasiness about your success. It is easy. Get in with the right people; use your family name and your distinguished ancestors; pull a few judicious advertising wires; do a few artistic stunts; get yourself into the papers long and often, no matter how; make yourself a fad; become a pet of the social autocrats—and your fame is assured. And—you will be what I am."

The young man, quietly ignoring the humor of the novelist's words, said protestingly, "But, surely, to portray human nature is legitimate art, Mr. Lagrange. Your great artists that the West is to produce will not necessarily be landscape painters or write essays upon nature, will they?"

"To portray human nature is legitimate work for an artist, yes"—agreed the novelist—"but he must portray human nature plus. The forces that shape human nature are the forces that must be felt in the picture and in the story. That these determining forces are so seldom seen by the eyes of the world, is the reason for pictures and stories. The artist who fails to realize for his world the character-creating elements in the life which he essays to paint or write, fails, to just that degree, in being an artist; or is self-branded by his work as criminally careless, a charlatan or a liar. That one who, for a price, presents a picture or a story without regard for the influence of his production upon the characters of those who receive it, commits a crime for which human law provides no adequate punishment. Being the famous Conrad Lagrange, you understand, I have the right to say this. You will probably believe it, some day—if you do not now. That is, you will believe it if you have the soul and the intelligence of an artist—if you have not—it will not matter—and you will be happy in your success."

As the novelist finished speaking, the two men arrived at the hotel steps, where they halted, with that indecision of chance acquaintances who have no plans beyond the passing moment, yet who, in mutual interest, would extend the time of their brief companionship. While they stood there, each hesitating to make the advance, a big touring car rolled up the driveway, and stopped under the full light of the veranda. Aaron King recognized the lady of the observation car platform, with her two traveling companions and the heavy-faced man who had met them at the depot. As the party greeted the novelist and he returned their salutation, the artist turned away to find again the chair, where, an hour before, the strange character who was to play so large a part in his life and work had found him. The dog, Czar, as if preferring the companionship of the artist to the company of those who were engaging his master's attention, followed the young man.

From where he sat, the painter could see the tall, uncouth figure of the famous novelist standing beside the automobile, while the occupants of the car were, apparently, absorbingly interested in what he was saying. The beautiful face of the woman was brightly animated as she evidently took the lead in the conversation. The artist could see her laughing and shaking her head. Once, he even heard her speak the writer's name; whereupon, every lounger upon the veranda, within hearing, turned to observe the party with curious interest. Several times, the young man noted that she glanced in his direction, half inquiringly, with a suggestion of being pleased, as though she were glad to have seen him in company with her celebrated friend. Then the man who held so large a place in the eyes of the world drew back, lifting his hat; the automobile started forward; the party called, "Good night." The woman's voice rose clear—so that the spectators might easily understand—"Remember, Mr. Lagrange—I shall expect you Thursday—day after to-morrow."

As Conrad Lagrange came up the hotel steps, the eyes of all were upon him; but he—apparently unconscious of the company—went straight to the artist; where, without a word, he dropped into the vacant chair by the young man's side, and began thoughtfully refilling his brier pipe. Flipping the match over the veranda railing, and expelling a prodigious cloud of smoke, the novelist said grimly, "And there—my fellow artist—go your masters. I trust you observed them with proper reverence. I would have introduced you, but I do not like to take the initiative in such outrages. That will come soon enough. The young should be permitted to enjoy their freedom while they may."

Aaron King laughed. "Thank you for your consideration," he returned, "but I do not think I am in any immediate danger."

"Which"—the other retorted dryly—"betrays either innocence, caution, or an unusual understanding of life. I am not, now, prepared to say whether you know too much or too little."

"I confess to a degree of curiosity," said the artist. "I traveled in the same Pullman with three of the party. May I ask the names of your friends?"

The other answered in his bitterest vein; "I have no friends, Mr. King—I have only admirers. As for their names"—he continued—"there is no reason why I should withhold either who they are or what they are. Besides, I observed that the reigning 'Goddess' in the realm of 'Modern Art' has her eye upon you, already. As I shall very soon be commanded to drag you to her 'Court,' it is well for you to be prepared."

The young man laughed as the other paused to puff vigorously at his brier pipe.

"That red-faced, bull-necked brute, is James Rutlidge, the son and heir of old Jim Rutlidge," continued the novelist. "Jim inherited a few odd millions from his father, and killed himself spending them in unmentionable ways. The son is most worthily carrying out his father's mission, with bright prospects of exceeding his distinguished parent's fondest dreams. But, unfortunately, he is hampered by lack of adequate capital—the bulk of the family wealth having gone with the old man."

"Do you mean James Rutlidge—the great critic?" exclaimed Aaron King, with increased interest.

"The same," answered the other, with his twisted smile. "I thought you would recognize his name. As an artist, you will undoubtedly have much to do with him. His friendship is one of the things that are vital to your success. Believe me, his power in modern art is a red-faced, bull-necked power that you will do well to recognize. Of his companions," he went on, "the horrible example is Edward J. Taine—friend and fellow martyr of James Rutlidge, Senior. Satan, perhaps, can explain how he has managed to outlive his partner. His home is in New York, but he has a big house on Fairlands Heights, with large orange groves in this district. He comes here winters for his health. He'll die before long. The effervescing young creature is his daughter, Louise—by his first wife. The 'Goddess'—who is not much older than his daughter—is the present Mrs. Taine."

"His wife!"

The artist's exclamation drew a sarcastic chuckle from the other. "I am prepared, now, to testify to your unworldly innocence of heart and mind," he gibed. "And, pray, why not his wife? You see, she was the ward of old Rutlidge—a niece, it is said. Mrs. Rutlidge—as you have no doubt heard—killed herself. It was shortly after her death that Jim took this little one into his home. She and young Jim grew up together. What was more natural or fitting than that her guardian—when he was about to depart from this sad world where human flesh is not able to endure an unlimited amount of dissipation—should give the girl as a lively souvenir to his bosom friend and companion of his unmentionable deviltries? The transaction also enabled him, you understand, to draw upon the Taine millions; and so permitted him to finish his distinguished career with credit. You, with your artist's extravagant fancy, have, no doubt, been thinking of her as fashioned for love. I assure you she knows better. The world in which she has been schooled has left her no hazy ideas as to what she was made for."

"I have heard of the Taines," said the younger man, thoughtfully. "I suppose this is the same family. They are very prominent in the social world, and quite generous patrons of the arts?"

"In the eyes of the world," said the novelist, "they are the noblest of our Nobility. They dwell in the rarefied atmosphere of millions. By the dollarless multitudes they are envied. They assume to be the cultured of the cultured. Patrons of the arts! Why, man, they have autographed copies of all my books! They and their kind feed me and my kind. They will feed you, sir, or by God you'll starve! But you need have no fear that the crust of genius will be your portion," he added meaningly. "As I remarked—the 'Goddess' has her eye upon you."

"And why do you so distinguish the lady?" asked the artist, quietly amused—with just a hint of well-bred condescension. "Has Mrs. Taine such powerful influence in the world of art?"

If Conrad Lagrange noticed his companion's manner he passed it by. "I perceive," he said, "that you are still somewhat lacking in the rudiments of your profession. The statement of faith adhered to by modern climbers on the ladder of fame—such as I have been, and you aspire to be—is that 'Pull' wins. Our creed is 'Graft.' By 'Influence' we stand, by 'Influence' we fall. It pleases Mrs. Taine to be, in the world of art, a lobbyist. She knows the insides of the inside rings and cliques and committees that say what is, and what is not, art; that declare who shall be, and who shall not be, artists. She has power with those who, in their might, grant position and place in the halls of fame; as their kinsmen in the political world pass the plums to those who court their favor. The great critics who thunder anathemas at the poor devils who are outside, eat out of her hand. Jim Rutlidge and his unholy crew are at her beck and call. Jim, you see, needing all he can get of the Taine millions, hopes to marry Louise. You can scarcely blame the young and beautiful Mrs. Taine for not being interested in her husband—who is going to die so soon. The poor girl must have some amusement, so she interests herself in art, don't you know. She gives more dinners to artists and critics; buys more pictures and causes more pictures to be bought; mothers more art-culture clubs; discovers more new and startling geniuses; in short, has a larger and better trained company of lions than any one else in the business. She deals in lions. It's her fad to collect them—same as others collect butterflies or postage stamps. She has one other fad that is less harmful and just as deceptive—a carefully nourished reputation for prudery. I sometimes think the Gods must laugh or choke. That woman would no more speak to you without a proper introduction than she would appear on the street without shoes or stockings. She has never been seen in an evening gown. Her beautiful shoulders have never been immodestly bared to the eyes of the world."

The artist thought of that moment on the observation car platform.

Presently, the novelist—refilling his pipe—said whimsically, "Some day, Mr. King, I shall write a true story. It shall be a novel of to-day, with characters drawn from life; and these characters, in my story, shall bear the names of the forces that have made them what they are and which they, in turn, have come to represent. I mean those forces that are so coloring and shaping the life and thought of this age."

"That ought to be interesting," said the other, "but I am not quite sure that I understand."

"Probably you don't. You have not been thinking much of these things. You have your eye upon Fame, and that old witch lives in another direction. To illustrate—our bull-necked friend and illustrious critic, James Rutlidge, in my story, will be named 'Sensual.' His distinguished father was one 'Lust.' The horrible example, Mr. Edward Taine,—boon companion of 'Lust,'—is 'Materialism'."

"Good!" laughed the artist. "I see; go on. Who is the daughter of 'Materialism?'"

"'Ragtime'," promptly returned the novelist, with a grin. "Who else could she be?"

"And Mrs. Taine?" urged the other.

The novelist responded quickly; "Why, the reigning 'Goddess' in the realm of 'Modern Art,' is 'The Age,' of course. Do you see? 'The Age' given over to 'Materialism' for base purposes by his companion, 'Lust.' And you—" he paused.

"Go on," cried the young man, "who or what am I in your story?"

"You, sir,"—answered Conrad Lagrange, seriously,—"in my story of modern life, represent Art. It remains to be seen whether 'The Age' will add you to her collection, or whether some other influence will intervene."

"And you"—persisted the artist—"surely you are in the story."

"I am very much in the story," the other answered. "My name is 'Civilization.' My story will be published when I am dead. I have a reputation to sustain, you know."

Aaron King was not laughing, now. Something, that lay deep hidden beneath the rude exterior of the man, made itself felt in his deep voice. Some powerful force, underlying his whimsical words, gripped the artist's mind—compelling him to search for hidden meanings in the novelist's fanciful suggestions.

A few moments passed in silence before the young man said slowly, "I met a character, yesterday, Mr. Lagrange, that might be added to your cast."

"There are several that will be added to my cast," the other answered dryly.

To which the painter returned, "Did you notice that woman with the disfigured face, at the depot?"

Conrad Lagrange looked at his companion, quickly. "Yes."

"Do you know her?" questioned the artist.

"No. Why do you ask?"

"Only because she interested me, and because she seemed to know your friends—Mr. Rutlidge and Mrs. Taine."

The novelist knocked the ashes from his pipe by tapping it on the veranda railing. The action seemed to express a peculiar mental effort; as though he were striving to recall something that had gone from his memory. "I saw what happened at the depot, of course," he said slowly. "I have seen the woman before. She lives here in Fairlands. Her name is Miss Willard. No one seems to know much about her. I can't get over the impression that I ought to know her—that I have met and known her somewhere years ago. Her manner, yesterday, at seeing Mrs. Taine, was certainly very strange." As if to free his mind from the unsuccessful effort to remember, he rose to his feet. "But why should she be added to the characters in my novel, Mr. King? What does she represent?"

"Her name,"—said the artist,—"in your study of life, is suggested by her face—so beautiful on the one side—so distorted on the other—her name should be 'Symbol'."

"There really is hope for you," returned the older man, with his quizzing smile. "Good night. Come, Czar." He passed into the hotel—the dog at his heels.

It was two days later—Thursday—that Conrad Lagrange made his memorable visit to the Taines—memorable, in my story, because, at that time, Mrs. Taine gave such unmistakable evidence of her interest in Aaron King and his future.

Chapter IV

At the House on Fairlands Heights

As my friend the social scientist would say; it is a phenomenon peculiar to urban life, that the social strata are more or less clearly defined geographically.

That is,—in the English of everyday,—people of different classes live in different parts of the city. As certain streets and blocks are given to the wholesale establishments, others to retail stores, and still others to the manufacturing plants; so there are the tenement districts, the slums, and the streets where may be found the homes of wealth and fashion.

In Fairlands, the social rating is largely marked by altitude. The city, lying in the lap of the hills and looking a little down upon the valley—plebeian business together with those who do the work of Fairlands occupies the lowest levels in the corporate limits. The heights are held by Fairlands' Pride.

Between these two extremes, the Fairlanders are graded fairly by the levels they occupy. It is most gratifying to observe how generally the citizens of this fortunate community aspire to higher things; and to note that the peculiarly proud spirit of this people is undoubtedly explained by this happy arrangement which enables every one to look down upon his neighbor.

The view from the winter home of the Taines was magnificent.

From the window of the room where Mrs. Taine sat, that afternoon, one could have looked down upon all Fairlands. One might, indeed, have done better than that. Looking over the wealth of semi-tropical foliage that—save for the tower of the red-brick Y.M.C.A. building, the white, municipal flagstaff, and the steeples and belfries of the churches—hid the city, one might have looked up at the mountains. High, high, above the low levels occupied by the hill-climbing Fairlanders, the mountains lift their heads in solemn dignity; looking down upon the loftiest Fairlander of them all—looking down upon even the Taines themselves.

But the glory of Mrs. Taine's God was not declared by the mountains. She sat by the window, indeed, but her eyes were upon the open pages of a book—a popular novel that by some strange legal lapse of the governmental conscience was—and is still—permitted in print.

The author of the story that so engrossed Mrs. Taine was—in her opinion—almost as great in literature as Conrad Lagrange, himself. By those in authority who pronounce upon the worthiness or the unworthiness of writer folk, he is, to-day, said to be one of the greatest writers of his generation. He is a realist—a modern of the moderns. His pen has never been debased by an inartistic and antiquated idealism. His claim to genius rests securely upon the fact that he has no ideals. He writes for that select circle of leaders who, like the Taines and the Rutlidges, are capable of appreciating his art. All of which means that he tells filthy stories in good English. That his stories are identical in material and motive with the vile yarns that are permitted only in the lowest class barber shops and in disreputable bar-rooms, in no way detracts from the admiring praise of his critics, the generosity of his publishers, or the appreciation of those for whom he writes.

With tottering step and feeble, shaking limbs, Edward Taine entered the apartment. As he stood, silently looking at his young wife, his glazed, red-rimmed eyes fed upon her voluptuous beauty with a look of sullen, impotent lustfulness that was near insanity. A spasm of coughing seized him; he gasped and choked, his wasted body shaken and racked, his dissipated face hideously distorted by the violence of the paroxysm. Wrecked by the flesh he had lived to gratify, he was now the mocked and tortured slave of the very devils of unholy passion that he had so often invoked to serve him. Repulsive as he was, he was an object to awaken the deepest pity.

Mrs. Taine, looking up from her novel, watched him curiously—without moving or changing her attitude of luxurious repose—without speaking. Almost, one would have said, a shade of a smile was upon her too perfect features.

When the man—who had dropped weak and exhausted into a chair—could speak, he glared at her in a pitiful rage, and, in his throaty whisper, said with a curse, "You seem to be amused."

Still, she did not speak. A tantalizing smile broke over her face, and she stretched her beautiful body lazily in her chair, as a well-conditioned animal stirs in sleek, physical contentment.

Again, with curses, he said, "I'm glad you so enjoy my company. To be laughed at, even, is better than your damned indifference."

"You misjudge me," she answered in a voice that, low and soft, was still richly colored by the wealth of vitality that found expression in her splendid body. "I am not at all indifferent to your condition—quite the contrary. I am intensely interested. As for the amusement you afford me—please consider—for three years I have amused you. Can you deny me my turn?"

He laughed with a hideously mirthless chuckle as he returned with ghastly humor, "I have had the worth of my money. I advise you to make the most of your opportunity. I shall make things as pleasant for you as I can, while I am with you, but, as you know, I am liable to leave you at any time, now."

"Pray don't hurry away," she replied sweetly. "I shall miss you so when you are gone."

He glared at her while she laughed mockingly.

"Where is everybody?" he asked. "The place is as lonely as a tomb."

"Louise is out riding with Jim."

"And what are you doing at home?" he demanded suspiciously.

"Me? Oh I remained to care for you—to keep you from being lonely."

"You lie. You are expecting some one."

She laughed.

"Who is it this time?" he persisted.

"Your insinuations are so unwarranted," she murmured.

"Whom are you expecting?"

"Dear me! how persistently you look for evil," she mocked. "You know perfectly well that, thanks to my tact, I am considered quite the model wife. You really should cultivate a more trusting disposition."

Another fit of coughing seized him, and while he suffered she again watched him with that curious air of interest. When he could command his voice, he gasped in a choking whisper, "You fiend! I know, and you know that I know. Am I so innocent that Jack Hanover, and Charlie Rodgers, and Black Whitman, and as many more of their kind, can make love to you under my very nose without my knowing it? You take damned good care—posing as a prude with your fad about immodest dress—that the world sees nothing; but you have never troubled to hide it from me."

Deliberately, she arose and stood before him. "And why should I trouble to hide anything from you?" she demanded. "Look at me"—she posed as if to exhibit for his critical inspection the charm of her physical beauty—"Look at me; am I to waste all this upon you? You tell me that you have had your money's worth—surely, the purchase price is mine to spend as I will. Even suppose that I were as evil as your foul mind sees me, what right have you to object? Are you so chaste that you dare cast a stone at me? Am I to have no pleasure in this hell you have made for me but the horrible pleasure of watching you in the hell you have made for yourself? Be satisfied that the world does not see your shame—though it's from no consideration of you, but wholly for myself, that I am careful. As for my modesty—you know it is not a fad but a necessity."

"That is just it"—he retorted—"it is the way you make a fad of a necessity! Forced to hide your shoulders, you make a virtue of concealment. You make capital of the very thing of which you are ashamed."

"And is not that exactly what we all do?" she asked with brutal cynicism. "Do you not fear the eyes of the world as much as I? Be satisfied that I play the game of respectability with you—that I give the world no cause for talk. You may as well be," she finished with devilish frankness, "for you are past helping yourself in the matter."

As she finished, a servant appeared to announce Mr. Conrad Lagrange; and the tall, uncouth figure of the novelist stood framed in the doorway; his sharp eyes regarding them with that peculiar, quizzing, baffling look.

Edward Taine laughed with that horrid chuckle. "Howdy-do, Lagrange—glad to see you."

Mrs. Taine went forward to greet the caller; saying as she gave him her hand, "You arrived just in time, Mr. Lagrange; Edward and I were discussing your latest book. We think it a masterpiece of realistic fiction. I'm sure it will add immensely to your fame. I hear it talked of everywhere as the most popular novel of the year. You wonderful man! How do you do it?"

"I don't do it," answered Conrad Lagrange, looking straight into her eyes. "It does itself. My books are really true products of the age that reads them; and—to paraphrase a statesman who was himself a product of his age—for those who read my books they are just the kind of books that I would expect such people to read."

Mrs. Taine looked at him with a curious, half-doubtful half-wistful expression; as though she glimpsed a hint of a meaning that did not appear upon the surface of his words. "You do say such—such—twisty things," she murmured. "I don't think I always understand what you mean; but when you look at me that way, I feel as though my maid had neglected to finish hooking me up."

The novelist bowed in mock gallantry—a movement which made his ungainly form appear more grotesque than ever. "Indeed, madam, to my humble eyes, you are most beautifully and fittingly—ah—hooked up." He turned toward the invalid. "And how is the fortunate husband of the charming Mrs. Taine to-day?"

"Fine, Lagrange, fine," said the man—a cough interrupting his words. "Really, I think that Gertrude is unduly alarmed about my condition. In this glorious climate, I feel like a three-year-old."

"You are looking quite like yourself," returned the novelist.

"There's nothing at all the matter with me but a slight bronchial trouble," continued the other, coughing again. Then, to his wife—"Dearest, won't you ring, please; I'm sure it's time for my toddy; perhaps Mr. Lagrange will join me in a drink. What'll it be, Lagrange?"

"Nothing, thanks, at this hour."

"No? But you'll pardon me, I'm sure—Doctor's orders you know."

A servant appeared. Mrs. Taine took the glass and carried it to her husband with her own hand, saying with tender solicitude, "Don't you think, dear, that you should lie down for a while? Mr. Lagrange will remain for dinner, you know. You must not tire yourself. I'm sure he will excuse you. I'll manage somehow to amuse him until Jim and Louise return."

"I believe I will rest a little, Gertrude." He turned to the guest—"While there is nothing really wrong, you know, Lagrange, still it's best to be on the safe side."

"By all means," said the novelist, heartily. "You should take care of yourself. Don't, I beg, permit me to detain you."

Mrs. Taine, with careful tenderness, accompanied her husband to the door. When he had passed from the room, she faced the novelist, with—"Don't you think Edward is really very much worse, Mr. Lagrange? I keep up appearances, you know, but—" she paused with a charming air of perplexed and worried anxiety.

"Your husband is certainly not a well man, madam—but you keep up appearances wonderfully. I really don't see how you manage it. But I suppose that for one of your nature it is natural."

Again, she received his words with that look of doubtful understanding—as though sensing some meaning beneath the polite, commonplace surface. Then, as if to lead away from the subject—"You must really tell me what you think of our California home. I told you in New York, you remember, that I should ask you, the first thing. We were so sorry to have missed you last year. Please be frank. Isn't it beautiful?"

"Very beautiful"—he answered—"exquisite taste—perfect harmony with modern art." His quizzing eyes twinkled, and a caricature of a smile distorted his face. "It fairly smells to heaven of the flesh pots."

She laughed merrily. "The odor should not be unfamiliar to you," she retorted. "By all accounts, your royalties are making you immensely rich. How wonderful it must be to be famous—to know that the whole world is talking about you! And that reminds me—who is your distinguished looking friend at the hotel? I was dying to ask you, the other night, but didn't dare. I know he is somebody famous."

Conrad Lagrange, studying her face, answered reluctantly, "No, he is not famous; but I fear he is going to be."

"Another twisty saying," she retorted. "But I mean to have an answer, so you may as well speak plainly. Have you known him long? What is his name? And what is he—a writer?"

"His name is Aaron King. His mother and I grew up in the same neighborhood. He is an artist."

"How romantic! Do you mean that he belongs to that old family of New England Kings?"

"He is the last of them. His father was Aaron King—a prominent lawyer and politician in his state."

"Oh, yes! I remember! Wasn't there something whispered at the time of his death—some scandal that was hushed up—money stolen—or something? What was it? I can't think."

"Whatever it was, Mrs. Taine, the son had nothing to do with it. Don't you think we might let the dead man stay safely buried?" There was an ominous glint in Conrad Lagrange's eyes.

Mrs. Taine answered hurriedly, "Indeed, yes, Mr. Lagrange. You are right. And you shall bring Mr. King out to see me. If he is as nice as he looks, I promise you I will be very good to him. Perhaps I may even help him a little, through Jim, you know—bring him in touch with the right people and that sort of thing. What does he paint?"

"Portraits." The novelist's tone was curt.

"Then I am sure I could do a great deal for him."

"And I am sure you would do a great deal to him," said Conrad Lagrange, bluntly.

She laughed again. "And just what do you mean by that, Mr. Lagrange? I'm not sure whether it is complimentary or otherwise."

"That depends upon what you consider complimentary," retorted the other. "As I told you—Aaron King is an artist."

Again, she favored him with that look of doubtful understanding; shaking her head with mock sadness, and making a long sigh. "Another twister"—she said woefully—"just when we were getting along so beautifully, too. Won't you try again?"

"In words of one syllable then—let him alone. He is, to-day, exactly where I was twenty years ago. For God's sake, let him alone. Play your game with those who are no loss to the world; or with those who, like me, are already lost. Let this man do his work. Don't make him what I am."

"Oh dear, oh dear," she laughed, "and these are words of one syllable! You talk as though I were a dreadful dragon seeking a genius to devour!"

"You are," said the novelist, gruffly.

"How nice. I'm all shivery with delight, already. You really must bring him now, you see. You might as well, for, if you don't, I'll manage some other way when you are not around to protect him. You don't want to trust him to me unprotected, do you?"

"No, and I won't," retorted Conrad Lagrange—which, though Mrs. Taine did not remark it, was also a twister.

"But after all, perhaps he won't come," she said with mock anxiety.

"Don't worry madam—he's just as much a fool as the rest of us."

As the novelist spoke, they heard the voices of Miss Taine and her escort, James Rutlidge. Mrs. Taine had only time to shake a finger in playful warning at her companion, and to whisper, "Mind you bring your artist to me, or I'll get him when you're not looking; and listen, don't tell Jim about him; I must see what he is like, first."

At lunch, the next day, Conrad Lagrange greeted the artist in his bitterest humor. "And how is the famous Aaron King, to-day? I trust that the greatest portrait painter of the age is well; that the hotel people have been properly attentive to the comfort of their illustrious guest? The world of art can ill afford to have its rarest genius suffer from any lack of the service that is due his greatness."

The young man's face flushed at his companion's mocking tone; but he laughed. "I missed you at breakfast."

"I was sleeping off the effect of my intellectual debauch—it takes time to recover from a dinner with 'Materialism,' 'Sensual,' 'Ragtime' and 'The Age'," the other returned, the menu in his hand. "What slop are they offering to put in our troughs for this noon's feed?"

Again, Aaron King laughed. But as the novelist, with characteristic comments and instructions to the waitress, ordered his lunch, the artist watched him as though waiting with interest his further remarks on the subject of his evening with the Taines.

When the girl was gone, Conrad Lagrange turned again to his companion, and from under his scowling brows regarded him much as a withered scientist might regard an interesting insect under his glass. "Permit me to congratulate you," he said suggestively—as though the bug had succeeded in acting in some manner fully expected by the scientist but wholly disgusting to him.

The artist colored again as he returned curiously, "Upon what?"

"Upon the start you have made toward the goal you hope to reach."

"What do you mean?"

"Mrs. Taine wants you."

"You are pleased to be facetious." Under the eyes of his companion, Aaron King felt that his reply did not at all conceal his satisfaction.

"I am pleased to be exact. I repeat—Mrs. Taine wants you. I am ordered by the reigning 'Goddess' of 'Modern Art'—'The Age'—to bring you into her 'Court.' You have won favor in her sight. She finds you good to look at. She hopes to find you—as good as you look. If you do not disappoint her, your fame is assured."

"Nonsense," said the artist, somewhat sharply; nettled by the obvious meaning and by the sneering sarcasm of the novelist's words and tone.

To which the other returned suggestively, "It is precisely because you can say, 'nonsense,' when you know it is no nonsense at all, but the exact truth, that your chance for fame is so good, my friend."

"And did some reigning 'Goddess' insure your success and fame?"

The older man turned his peculiar, penetrating, baffling eyes full upon his companion's face, and in a voice full of cynical sadness answered, "Exactly so. I paid court to the powers that be. They gave me the reward I sought; and—they made me what I am."

So it came about that Conrad Lagrange, in due time, introduced Aaron King to the house on Fairlands Heights. Or,—as the novelist put it,—he, "Civilization",—in obedience to the commands of her "Royal Highness", "The Age",—presented the artist at her "Majesty's Court"; that the young man might sue for the royal favor.

It was, perhaps, a month after the presentation ceremony, that the painter made what—to him, at least—was an important announcement.

Chapter V

The Mystery of the Rose Garden

The acquaintance of Aaron King and Conrad Lagrange had developed rapidly into friendship.

The man whom the world had chosen to place upon one of the highest pinnacles of its literary favor, and who—through some queer twist in his nature—was so lonely and embittered by his exaltation, seemed to find in the younger man who stood with the crowd at the foot of the ladder, something that marked him as different from his fellows.

Whether it was the artist's mother; some sacredly hidden memories of Lagrange's past; or, perhaps, some fancied recognition of the artist's genius and its possibilities; the strange man gave no hint; but he constantly sought the company of Aaron King, with an openness that made his preference for the painter's society very evident. If he had said anything about it, at all, Conrad Lagrange, likely, would have accounted for his interest, upon the ground that his dog, Czar, found the companionship agreeable. Their friendship, meanwhile—in the eyes of the world—conferred a peculiar distinction upon the young man—a distinction not at all displeasing to the ambitious artist; and the value of which he, probably, overrated.

To Aaron King—aside from the subtle flattery of the famous novelist's attention—there was in the personality of the odd character a something that appealed to him with peculiar strength. Perhaps it was that the man's words, so often sharp and stinging with bitter sarcasm, seemed always to carry a hidden meaning that gave, as it were, glimpses of another nature buried deeply beneath a wreck of ruined dreams and disappointing achievements. Or, it may have been that, under all the cruel, world-hardness of the thoughts expressed, the young man sensed an undertone of pathetic sadness. Or, again, perhaps, it was those rare moments, when—on some walk that carried them beyond the outskirts of the town, and brought the mountains into unobstructed view—the clouds of bitterness were lifted; and the man spoke with poetic feeling of the realities of life, and of the true glory and mission of the arts; counseling his friend with an intelligence as true and delicate as it was rare and fine.

It was nearly two months after Conrad Lagrange had introduced the young man at the house on Fairlands Heights. The hour was late. The painter—returning from a dinner and an evening at the Taine home—found the novelist, with pipe and dog, in a deserted corner of the hotel veranda. Dropping into the chair that was placed as if it awaited his coming, the artist—with no word of greeting to the man—bent over the brown head that was thrust so insistently against his knee, as Czar, with gently waving tail, made him welcome. Looking affectionately into the brown eyes while he stroked the silky coat, the young man answered in the language that all dogs understand; while the novelist, from under his scowling brows, regarded the two intently.

"They were disappointed that you were not there," said the painter, presently. "Mrs. Taine, particularly, charged me to say that she will not forgive, until you do proper penance for your sin."

"I had better company," retorted the other. "Czar and I went for a look at the mountains. I suppose you have noticed that Czar does not care for the Fairlands Heights crowd. He is very peculiar in his friendships—for a dog. His instincts are remarkable."

At the sound of his name, Czar transferred his attentions, for a moment, to his master; then stretched himself in his accustomed place beside the novelist's chair.

The artist laughed. "I did my best to invent an acceptable excuse for you; but she said it was no use—nothing short of your own personal prayers for mercy would do."

"Humph; you should have reminded her that I purchased an indulgence some weeks ago."

Again, the other laughed shortly. Watching him closely, Conrad Lagrange said, in his most sneering tones, "I trust, young man, that you are not failing to make good use of your opportunities. Let's see—dinner and the evening five times—afternoon calls as many—with motor trips to points of interest—and one theater party to Los Angeles—believe me; it is not often that struggling genius is so rewarded—before it has accomplished anything bad enough to merit such attention."

"I have been idling most shamefully, haven't I?" said the artist.

"Idling!" rasped the other. "You have been the busiest hay-maker in the land. These scientific, intensive cultivation farmers of California are not in your class when it comes to utilizing the sunshine. Take my advice and continue your present activity without bothering yourself by any sentimental thoughts of your palette and brushes. The mere vulgar tools of your craft are of minor importance to one of your genius and opportunity."

Then, in a half embarrassed manner, Aaron King made his announcement. "That may all be," he said, "but just the same, I am going to work."

"I knew it"—returned the other, in mocking triumph—"I knew it the moment you came up the steps there. I could tell it by your walk; by the air with which you carried yourself; by your manner, your voice, your laugh—you fairly reek of prosperity and achievement—you are going to paint her portrait."

"And why not?" retorted the young man, rather sharply, a trifle nettled by the other's tone.

"Why not, indeed!" murmured the novelist. "Indeed, yes—by all means! It is so exactly the right thing to do that it is startling. You scale the heights of fame with such confident certainty in every move that it is positively uncanny to watch you."

"If one's work is true, I fail to see why one should not take advantage of any influence that can contribute to his success," said the painter. "I assure you I am not so wealthy that I can afford to refuse such an attractive commission. You must admit that the beautiful Mrs. Taine is a subject worthy the brush of any artist; and I suppose it is conceivable that I might be ambitious to make a genuinely good job of it."

The older man, as though touched by the evident sincerity of the artist's words, dropped his sneering tone and spoke earnestly; "The beautiful Mrs. Taine is a subject worthy a master's brush, my friend. But take my word for it, if you paint her portrait as a master would paint it, you will sign your own death warrant—so far as your popularity and fame as an artist goes."

"I don't believe it," declared Aaron King, flatly.

"I know you don't. If you did, and still accepted the commission, you wouldn't be fit to associate with honest dogs like Czar, here."

"But why"—persisted the artist—"why do you insist that my portrait of Mrs. Taine will be disastrous to my success, just to the degree that it is a work of genuine merit?"

To which the novelist answered, cryptically, "If you have not the eyes to see the reason, it will matter little whether you know it or not. If you do see the reason, and, still, produce a portrait that pleases your sitter, then you will have paid the price; you will receive your reward; and"—the speaker's tone grew sad and bitter—"you will be what I am."

With this, he arose abruptly and, without another word, stalked into the hotel; the dog following with quiet dignity, at his heels.

From the beginning of their acquaintance, almost, the novelist and the artist had dropped into the habit of taking their meals together. At breakfast, the next morning, Conrad Lagrange reopened the conversation he had so abruptly closed the night before. "I suppose," he said, "that you will set up a studio, and do the thing in proper style?"

"Mrs. Taine told me of a place that is for rent, and that she thinks would be just the thing," returned the young man. "It is across the road from that big grove owned by Mr. Taine. I was wondering if you would care to walk out that way with me this morning and help me look it over."

The older man's hearty acceptance of the invitation assured the artist of his genuine interest, and, an hour later—after Aaron King had interviewed the agent and secured the keys, with the privilege of inspecting the premises—the two set out together.

They found the place on the eastern edge of the town; half-hidden by the orange groves that surrounded it on every side. The height of the palms that grew along the road in front, the pepper and eucalyptus trees that overshadowed the house, and the size of the orange-trees that shut in the little yard with walls of green, marked the place as having been established before the wealth of the far-away East discovered the peculiar charm of the Fairlands hills. The lawn, the walks, and the drive were unkempt and overgrown with weeds. The house itself,—a small cottage with a wide porch across the front and on the side to the west,—unpainted for many seasons, was tinted by the brush of the elements, a soft and restful gray.

But the artist and his friend, as they approached, exclaimed aloud at the beauty of the scene; for, as if rejoicing in their freedom from restraint, the roses had claimed the dwelling, so neglected by man, as their own. Up every post of the porch they had climbed; over the porch roof, they spread their wealth of color; over the gables, screening the windows with graceful lattice of vine and branch and leaf and bloom; up to the ridge and over the cornice, to the roof of the house itself—even to the top of the chimney they had won their way—and there, as if in an ecstasy of wanton loveliness, flung, a spray of glorious, perfumed beauty high into the air.

On the front porch, the men turned to look away over the gentle slope of the orange groves, on the other side of the road, to the towering peaks and high ridges of the mountains—gleaming cold and white in the winter of their altitude. To the northeast, San Bernardino reared his head in lonely majesty—looking directly down upon the foothills and the feeble dwellers in the valley below. Far beyond, and surrounded by the higher ridges and peaks and canyons of the range, San Gorgonio sat enthroned in the skies—the ruler of them all. From the northeast, westward, they viewed the mighty sweep of the main range to Cajon Pass and the San Gabriels, beyond, with San Antonio, Cucamonga, and their sister peaks lifting their heads above their fellows. In the immediate landscape, no house or building was to be seen. The dark-green mass of the orange groves hid every work of man's building between them and the tawny foothills save the gable and chimney of a neighboring cottage on the west.

"Listen"—said Conrad Lagrange, in a low tone, moved as always by the grandeur and beauty of the scene—"listen! Don't you hear them calling? Don't you feel the mountains sending their message to these poor insects who squirm and wriggle in this bit of muck men call their world? God, man! if only we, in our work, would heed the message of the hills!"

The novelist spoke with such intensity of feeling—with such bitter sadness and regret in his voice—that Aaron King could not reply.

Turning, the artist unlocked the door, and they entered the cottage.

They found the interior of the house well arranged, and not in bad repair. "Just the thing for a bachelor's housekeeping"—was the painter's verdict—"but for a studio—impossible," and there was a touch of regret in his voice.

"Let's continue our exploration," said the novelist, hopefully. "There's a barn out there." And they went out of the house, and down the drive on the eastern side of the yard.

Here, again, they saw the roses in full possession of the place—by man, deserted. From foundation to roof, the building—a small simple structure—was almost hidden under a mass of vines. There was one large room below; with a loft above. The stable was in the rear. Built, evidently, at a later date than the house, the building was in better repair. The walls, so hidden without by the roses, were well sided; the floors were well laid. The big, sliding, main door opened on the drive in front; between it and the corner, to the west, was a small door; and in the western end, a window.

Looking curiously from this window, Conrad Lagrange uttered an exclamation, and hurried abruptly from the building. The artist followed.

From the end of the barn, and extending, the full width of the building, to the west line of the yard, was a rose garden—such a garden as Aaron King had never seen. On three sides, the little plot was enclosed by a tall hedge of Ragged Robins; above the hedge, on the south and west, was the dark-green wall of the orange grove; on the north, the pepper and eucalyptus trees in the yard, and a view of the distant mountains; and on the east, the vine-hidden end of the barn. Against the southern wall,—and, so, directly opposite the trellised, vine-covered arch of the entrance,—a small, lattice bower, with a rustic table and seats within, was completely covered, as was the barn, by the magically woven tapestry of the flowers. In the corner of the hedge farthest from the entrance they found a narrow gate. Unlike the rest of the premises, the garden was in perfect order—the roses trimmed and cared for; the walks neatly edged and clean; with no weed or sign of untidiness or neglect anywhere.

The two men had come upon the spot so suddenly—so unexpectedly—the contrast with the neglected grounds and buildings was so marked—that they looked at each other in silence. The little retreat—so lovely, so hidden by its own beauty from the world, so cared for by careful hands—seemed haunted by an invisible spirit. Very quietly,—almost reverently,—they moved about; talking in low tones, as though half expecting—they knew not what.

"Some one loves this place," said the novelist, softly, when they stood, again, in the entrance.

And the artist answered in the same hushed voice, "I wonder what it means?"

When they were again in the barn, Aaron King became eagerly enthusiastic over the possibilities of the big room. "Some rightly toned burlap on the walls and ceiling,"—he pointed out,—"with floor covering and rugs in harmony; there"—rolling back the big door as he spoke—"your north light; some hangings and screens to hide the stairway to the loft, and the stable door; your entrance over here in the corner, nicely out of the way; and the window looking into the garden—it's great man, great!"

"And," answered Conrad Lagrange, from where he stood in the big front door, "the mountains! Don't forget the mountains. The soft, steady, north light on your canvas, and a message from the mountains to your soul, through the same window, should make it a good place to work, Mr. Painter-man. I suppose over here"—he moved away from the window, and spoke in his mocking way—"over here, you will have a tea-table for the ladies of the circle elect—who will come to, 'oh', and, 'ah', their admiration of the newly discovered genius, and to chatter their misunderstandings of his art. Of course, there will be a page in velvet and gold. By all means, get hold of an oriental kid of some kind—oriental junk is quite the rage this year. You should take advantage of every influence that can contribute to your success, you know. And, whatever you do, don't fail to consult the 'Goddess' about these essentials of your craft. Many a promising genius has been lost to fame, through inviting the wrong people to take tea in his studio. But"—he finished whimsically, looking from the window into the garden—"but what the devil do you suppose the spirit who lives out there will think about it all."

The days of the two following weeks were busy days for Aaron King. He leased the place in the orange groves, and set men to work making it habitable. The lawn and grounds were trimmed and put in order;

the interior of the house was renovated by painter and paper-hanger; and the barn, under the artist's direction, was transformed into an ideal studio. There was a trip to Los Angeles—quite fortunately upon a day when Mrs. Taine must go to the city shopping—for rugs and hangings; and another trip to purchase the tools of the artist's craft. And, at last, there was a Chinese cook and housekeeper to find; with supplies for his kitchen. It was at Conrad Lagrange's suggestion, that, from the first, every one was given strict orders to keep out of the rose garden.

Every day, the novelist—accompanied, always, by Czar—walked out that way to see how things were progressing; and often,—if he had not been too busy to notice,—Aaron King might have seen a look of wistfulness in the keen, baffling eyes of the famous man—so world-weary and sad. And, while he did not cease to mock and jeer and offer sarcastic advice to his younger friend, the touch of pathos—that, like a minor chord, was so often heard in his most caustic and cruel speeches—was more pronounced. As for Czar—he always returned to the hotel with evident reluctance; and managed to express, in his dog way, the thoughts his distinguished master would not put in words.

Very often, too, the big touring car from the house on Fairlands Heights stopped in front of the cottage, while the occupants inspected the premises, and—with many exclamations of flattering praise, and a few suggestions—made manifest their interest.

In time, it was finished and ready—from the big easel by the great, north window in the studio, to the white-jacketed Yee Kee in the kitchen. When the last workman was gone with his tools; and the two men, after looking about the place for an hour, were standing on the front porch; Conrad Lagrange said, "And the stage is set. The scene shifters are off. The audience is waiting. Ring up the curtain for the next act. Even Czar has looked upon everything and calls it good—heh Czar?"

The dog went to him; and, for some minutes, the novelist looked down into the brown eyes of his four-footed companion who seemed so to understand. Still fondling the dog,—without looking at the artist,—the older man continued, "You will have your things moved over in the morning, I suppose? Or, will we lunch together, once more?"

Aaron King laughed—as a boy who has prepared a surprise, and has been struggling manfully to keep the secret until the proper moment should arrive. Placing his hand on the older man's shoulder, he answered meaningly, "I had planned that we would move in the morning." At the other's puzzled expression he laughed again.

"We?" said the novelist, facing his friend, quickly.

"Come here," returned the other. "I must show you something you haven't seen."

He led the way to a room that they had decided he would not need, and the door of which was locked. Taking a key from his pocket, he handed it to his friend.

"What's this?" said the older man, looking foolishly at the key in his hand.

"It's the key to that door," returned the other, with a gleeful chuckle. Then—"Unlock it."

"Unlock it?"

"Sure—that's what I gave you the key for."

Conrad Lagrange obeyed. Through the open door, he saw, not the bare and empty room he supposed was there, but a bedroom—charmingly furnished, complete in every detail. Turning, he faced his companion silently, inquiringly—with a look that Aaron King had never before seen in those strange, baffling eyes.

"It's yours"—said the artist, hastily—"if you care to come. You'll have a free hand here, you know; for I will be in the studio much of the time. Kee will cook the things you like. You and Czar can come and go as you will. There is the arbor in the rose garden, you know, and see here"—he stepped to the window—"I chose this room for you, because it looks out upon your mountains."

The strange man stood at the window for, what seemed to the artist, a long time. Suddenly, he turned to say sharply, "Young man, why did you do this?"

"Why"—stammered the other, disconcerted—"because I want you—because I thought you would like to come. I beg your pardon—if I have made a mistake—but surely, no harm has been done."

"And you think you could stand living with me—for any length of time?"

The' painter laughed with relief. "Oh, that's it! I didn't know you had such a tender conscience. You scared me for a minute, I should think you would know by this time that you can't phase me with your wicked tongue."

The novelist's face twisted into a grotesque smile. "I warn you—I will flay you and your friends just the same. You need it for the good of your soul."

"As often and as hard as you like"—returned the other, heartily—"just so it's for the good of my soul. You will come?"

"You will permit me to stand my share of the expense?"

"Anything you like—if you will only come."

The older man said gently,—for the first time calling the artist by his given name,—"Aaron, I believe that you are the only person in the world who would, really want me; and I know that you are the only person in the world to whom I would be grateful for such an invitation."

The artist was about to reply, when the big automobile stopped in front of the house. Czar, on the porch, gave a low growl of disapproval; and, through the open door, they saw Mr. Taine and his wife with James Rutlidge and Louise.

The novelist said something, under his breath, that had a vicious sound—quite unlike his words of the moment before. Czar, in disgust, retreated to the shelter of Yee Kee's domain. With a laugh, the younger man went out to meet his friends.

"Are you at home this afternoon, Sir Artist?" called Mrs. Taine, gaily, as he went down the walk.

"I will always be at home to the right people," he answered, greeting the other members of the party.

As they moved toward the house,—Mr. Taine choking and coughing, his daughter chattering and exclaiming, and James Rutlidge critically observing,—Mrs. Taine dropped a little back to Aaron King's side. "And are you really established, at last?" she asked eagerly; with a charming, confidential air.

"We move to-morrow morning," he answered.

"We?" she questioned.

"Conrad Lagrange and I. He is going to live with me, you know."

"Oh!"

It is remarkable how much meaning a woman can crowd into that one small syllable; particularly, when she draws a little away from you as she speaks it.

"Why," he murmured apologetically, "don't you approve?"

Mrs. Taine's beautiful eyebrows went up inquiringly—"And why should I either approve or disapprove?"

The young man was saved by the arrival of his guests at the porch steps, and by the appearance of Conrad Lagrange, in the doorway.

"How delightful!" exclaimed Mrs. Taine, heartily; as she, in turn, greeted the famous novelist. "Mr. King was just telling me that you were going to share this dear little place with him. I quite envy you both."

The others had passed into the house.

"You are sometimes guilty of saying twisty things yourself, aren't you?" returned the man; and, as he spoke, his remarkable eyes were fixed upon her as though reading her innermost thoughts.

She flushed under his meaning gaze, but carried it off gaily with—"Oh dear! I wonder if my maid has hooked me up properly, this time?"

They left Mr. Taine in an easy chair, with a bottle of his favorite whisky; and went over the place—from the arbor in the rose garden to Yee Kee's pantry—Mr. Rutlidge, critically and authoritatively approving; Louise, effervescing the same sugary nothings at every step; Mrs. Taine, with a pretty air of proprietorship; Conrad Lagrange, thoughtfully watching; and Aaron King, himself, irresponsibly gay and boyishly proud as he exhibited his achievements.

In the studio, Mrs. Taine—standing before the big easel—demanded to know of the artist, when he would begin her portrait—she was so interested, so eager to begin—how soon could she come? Louise assumed a worshipful attitude, and, gazing at the young man with reverent eyes, waited breathlessly. James Rutlidge drew near, condescendingly attentive, to the center of attraction. Conrad Lagrange turned his back.

"Really," murmured the painter, "I hope you will not be too impatient, Mrs. Taine, I fear I cannot be ready for some time yet. I suppose I must confess to being over-sensitive to my environment; for it is a fact that my working mood does not come upon me readily amid strange surroundings. When I have become acclimated, as it were, I will be ready for you."

"How wonderful!" breathed Louise.

"Quite right," agreed Mr. Rutlidge.

"Whenever you are ready," said Mrs. Taine, submissively.

When their friends from the Heights were gone, Conrad Lagrange looked the artist up and down, as he said with cutting sarcasm, "You did that very nicely. Over-sensitive to your environment, hell! If you are a bit fine strung, you have no business to make a show of it. It's a weakness, not a virtue. And the man who makes capital out of any man's weakness,—even of his own,—is either a criminal or a fool or both."

Then they went back to the hotel for dinner.

The next morning, the artist and the novelist moved from the hotel, to establish themselves in the little house in the orange groves—the little house with its unobstructed view of the mountains, and with its rose garden, so mysteriously tended.

Chapter VI

An Unknown Friend

When Yee Kee announced lunch, the artist, the novelist, and the dog were settled in their new home. In the afternoon, the painter spent an hour or two fussing over portfolios of old sketches, in his studio; while Conrad Lagrange and Czar lounged on the front porch.

Once, the dog rose quietly, and, walking sedately to the edge of the porch toward the west, stood for some minutes gazing intently into the dark green mass of the orange grave. At last, as if concluding that whatever it was it was all right, he went calmly back to his place beside the novelist's chair.

"Do you know,"—said the artist, as they sat on the porch that evening, with their after-dinner pipes,—"I believe this old place is haunted."

"If it isn't, it ought to be," answered the other, contentedly—playing with Czar's silky ears. "A good ghost would fit in nicely here, wouldn't it—or he, or she. Its spookship would travel far to find a more delightful place for spooking in, and—providing, of course, she were a perfectly respectable hant—what a charming addition to our family he would make. When it was weary of moping and mowing and sobbing and wailing and gibbering, she could curl up at the foot of your bed and sleep; as Czar, here, curls up and sleeps at the foot of mine. A good ghost, you know—if he becomes really attached to you— is as constant and faithful and affectionate and companionable as a good dog."

"B-r-r-r," said the artist. And Czar turned to look at him, questioningly.

"All the same"—the painter continued—"when I was out there in the studio, I could feel some one watching me—you know the feeling."

Conrad Lagrange returned mockingly, "I trust your over-sensitive, artistic temperament is not to be so influenced by our ghostly visitor that you will be unfitted for your work."

The other laughed. Then he said seriously, "Joking aside, Lagrange, I feel a presentiment—I can't put it into words—but—I feel that I am going to begin the real work of my life right here. I"—he hesitated—"it seems to me that I can sense some influence that I can't define—it's the mystery of the rose garden, perhaps," he finished with another short laugh.

The man, who, in the eyes of the world, had won so large a measure of the success that his friend desired; and whose life was so embittered by the things for which he was envied by many; made no reply other than his slow, twisted smile.

Silently, they watched the purple shadows of the mountains deepen; and saw the outlines of the tawny foothills grow vague and dim, until they were lost in the dusky monotone of the evening. The last faint tint of sunset color went from the sky back of the San Gabriels; while, close to the mountain peaks and ridges, the stars came out. The rows and the contour of the orange groves could no longer be distinguished the forms of the nearby trees were lost—the rich, lustrous green of their foliage brushed out with the dull black of the night; while the twinkling lights of the distant towns and hamlets, in the valley below, shone as sparkling jewels on the inky, velvet robe that, fold on fold, lay over the landscape.

When the two had smoked in silence, for some time, the artist said slowly, "You knew my mother very well, did you not, Mr. Lagrange?"

"We were children together, Aaron." As he spoke, the man's deep voice was gentle, as always, when the young man's mother was mentioned.

Again, for a little, neither spoke. As they sat looking away to the mountains, each seemed occupied with his own thoughts. Yet each felt that the other, to a degree, understood what he, himself, was thinking.

Once more, the artist broke the silence,—facing his mother's friend with quiet resolution,—as though he felt himself forced to speak but knew not exactly how to begin. "Did you know her well—after—after my father's death—and while I was abroad?"

The other bowed his head—"Yes."

"Very well?"

"Very well."

As if at loss for words, Aaron King still hesitated. "Mr. Lagrange," he said, at last, "there are some things about—about mother—that I would like to tell you—that I think she would want me to tell you, under the circumstances."

"Yes," said Conrad Lagrange, gently.

"Well,—to begin,—you know, perhaps, how much mother and I have always been—" his fine voice broke and the older man bowed his head; but, with a slight lift of his determined chin, the painter went on calmly—"to each other. After father's death, until I was seventeen, we were never separated. She was my only teacher. Then I went away to school, seeing her only during my vacations, which we always spent, together in the country. Three years ago, I went abroad to finish my study. I did not see her again until—until I was called home."

"I know," came in low tones from the other.

"But, sir, while it seemed necessary that I should be away from home,—that we should be separated,—all through this period, we exchanged almost daily letters; planning for the future, and looking forward to the time when we could, again, be together."

"I know, Aaron. It was very unusual—and very beautiful."

"When we were together, before I went away, I was a mere lad," continued the artist. "I knew in a general way that father had been a successful lawyer, and quite prominent in politics; and—because there was no change in our manner of living after his death, and there seemed to be always money for whatever we wanted, I suppose—I assumed, thoughtlessly, that there would always be plenty. During the years while I was at school, there was never, in any way, the slightest hint in mother's letters that would lead me to question the abundance of her resources. When they called me home,—" his voice broke, "—I found my mother dying—almost in poverty—our home stripped of the art treasures she loved—her own room, even, empty of everything save the barest necessities." In bitter sorrow and shame, the young man buried his face in his hands.

The novelist, his gaunt features twitching with the emotion that even his long schooling in the tragedies of life could not suppress, waited silently.

When the artist had regained, in a measure, his self-control, he continued,—and every word came from him in shame and humiliation,—"Before she died, she told me about—my father. In the settlement of his affairs, at the time of his death, it appeared that he had taken advantage of the confidence of certain clients and had betrayed his trust; appropriating large sums to his own interests. He had even taken advantage of mother's influence in certain circles, and, relying upon her unquestioning faith in his integrity, had made her an unconscious instrument in furthering his schemes."

Conrad Lagrange made as if to speak, but checked himself and waited for the other to continue.

Aaron King went on; "Out of regard for my mother, the matter was kept as quiet as possible. The one who suffered the heaviest loss was able to protect her—in a measure. All the others were fully reimbursed. But mother—it would have been easier for her if she had died then. She withdrew from her friends and from the life she loved—she denied herself to all who sought her and devoted her life to me. Above all, she planned to keep me in ignorance of the truth until I should be equipped to win the place in the world that she coveted for me. It was for that, she sent me away, and kept me from home. As the demands for my educational expenses grew naturally heavier, she supplemented the slender resources, left in the final settlement of my father's estate, by sacrificing the treasures of her home, and by giving up the luxuries to which she had been accustomed from childhood. She even provided for me after her death—not wealth, but a comfortable amount, sufficient to support me in good circumstances until I can gain recognition and an income from my work."

Under the lash of his memories, the young man sprang to his feet.

"In God's name, Lagrange, why did not some one tell me? I did not know—I did not know—I thought—O mother, mother, mother—why did you do it? Why was I not told? All these years I have lived a selfish fool, and you—you—I would have given up everything—I would have worked in a ditch, rather than accept this."

The deep, quiet voice of Conrad Lagrange broke the stillness that followed the storm of the artist's passionate words. "And that is the answer, Aaron. She knew, too well, that you would not have accepted her sacrifice, if you had known. That is why she kept the secret until you had finished your education. She forbade her friends—she forbade me to interfere. And don't you see that she was right? Don't you see it? We would have done her the greatest injustice if we had, against her will, deprived her of this privilege. Her splendid pride, her high sense of honor, her nobility of spirit demanded the sacrifice. It was her right. God forgive me—I tried to make her see it otherwise—but she knew best. She always knew best, Aaron. Her only hope of regaining for you that self-respect and that position in life to which you—by right of birth and natural endowment—are entitled, was in you. The name which she had given to you could be restored to honor by you only. To train and equip you for your work, and to enable you, unhampered by need, to gain your footing, was the determined passion of her life. Her sacrifice, her suffering to that end, was the only restitution she could make to you for that which your father had squandered. Her proud spirit, her fine intelligence, her mother love for you, demanded it."

"I know," returned the artist. "She told me before she died. She made me understand. She said that it was my inheritance. She asked for my promise that I would be true to her purpose. Her last words were an expression of her confidence that I would not disappoint her—that I would win a place and name that would wipe out the shame of my father's dishonor. And I will, Lagrange, I must. Mother—mother shall not be disappointed—she shall not be disappointed."

"No,"—said the older man, so softly that the other, torn by the passion of his own thoughts, did not hear,—"No, Aaron, your mother will not be disappointed."

For a time longer they sat in silence. Then the young man said, "I wish I knew the name of my mother's friend—the one who suffered the heaviest loss through my father, and who so generously protected her in the crisis. I would like to thank him, at least. I begged her to tell me, but she would not. She said he would not want me to know—that for me to attempt to reimburse him would, to his mind, rob him of his real reward."

Conrad Lagrange, his head bowed, spoke quietly to the dog at his feet. Rising, Czar laid his soft muzzle on his master's knee and looked up into the homely, world-worn face. Gently, the strange man—so lonely and embittered in the fame that he had won—at a price—stroked the brown head. "Your mother knew best, Aaron," he said slowly, without looking at his companion. "You must believe that she knew best. Her beautiful spirit could not lead her astray. She was right in this, also. Your sentiment does you honor, but you must respect her wish. Whoever the man was—she had reasons, I am sure, for feeling as she did—that it would be better for you not to know. It was some one, perhaps, whose influence upon you, she had cause to fear."

"It was very strange," returned the artist, hesitatingly. "Perhaps I ought not to say it. But I felt that, as you suggest, she feared for me to know. She seemed to want to tell me, but did not, for my sake. It was very strange."

Conrad Lagrange made no reply.

"I wanted you to know about mother,"—continued the artist,—"because I would like you to understand why—why I must succeed in my work."

The older man smiled to himself, in the dusk. "I have always known why you must succeed, Aaron," he returned. "I have never questioned your motives. I question only your understanding of success. I question—if you will pardon me—your understanding of your mother's wish for you."

Then, in one of those rare momentary moods, when he seemed to reveal to his young friend his real nature that lay so deeply hidden from the world, he added, "You are right, Aaron. This place is haunted—haunted by the spirit of the mountains, yonder—haunted by the spirit of the rose garden, out there. The silent strength of the hills, and the loveliness of the garden will attend you in your studio, as you work. I do not wonder that you feel a presentiment that your artistic future is to be shaped here; for between these influences and the other influences that will be brought to bear upon you, you will be forced to decide. May the God of all true art and artists help you to make no mistake. Listen!"

As though in answer to the solemn words of the man who spoke from the fullness of a life-long experience and from the depths of a life-old love, a strain of music came from out the fragrant darkness. Somewhere, hidden in the depths of the orange grove, the soul of a true musician was seeking expression in the tones of a violin.

Softly, sadly, with poignant clearness, the music lifted into the night—low and pleadingly at first; then stronger and more vibrant with feeling, as though sweetly insistent in its call; swelling next in volume and passion, as though in warning of some threatening evil; ringing with loving fear; sobbing, wailing, moaning, in anguish; clearly, gloriously, triumphant, at last; then sinking into solemn, reverent benediction—losing itself, finally, in the darkness, even as it had come.

The two men, so fashioned by nature to receive such music, listened with emotions they could not have put into words. For the moment, the music to them was the voice of the guarding, calling, warning spirit of the mountains that, in their calm, majestic strength, were so far removed from the petty passions and longings of the baser world at their feet—it was the voice of the loving intimacy, the sweet purity, and the sacred beauty of the spirit of the garden. It was as though the things of which Conrad Lagrange had just spoken so reverently had cried aloud to them, out of the night, in confirmation of his words.

Chapter VII

Mrs. Taine in Quaker Gray

Aaron King seemed loth to begin his work on the portrait of Mrs. Taine. Day after day, without apparent reason, he put it off—spending the hours in wandering aimlessly about the place, idling on the porch, or doing nothing in his studio. He would start from the house to the building at the end of the rose garden, as though moved by some clearly defined purpose—and then, for an hour or more, would dawdle among the things of his craft, with irresolute mind—turning over his sketches and drawings with uncertain hands, as though searching for something he knew was not there; toying with his paints and brushes; or sitting before his empty easel, looking away through the big window to the distant mountains. He seemed incapable of fixing his mind upon the task to which he attached so much importance. Several times, Mrs. Taine called, but he begged her to be patient; and she, with pretended awe of the moods of genius, waited.

Conrad Lagrange jeered and mocked, offered sneering advice or sarcastic compliment; and, under it all, was keenly watchful and sympathetic— understanding better than the artist himself, perhaps, the secret of the painter's hesitation. Every day,—sometimes in the morning, sometimes in the afternoon or evening unseen musician, in the orange grove wrought for them melodie that, whether grave or gay, always carried, somehow, the feeling that had so moved them in the mysterious darkness of that first evening.

They knew, now, of course, that the musician lived in the neighboring house—the gable and chimney of which was just visible above the orange-trees. But that was all. Obedient to some whimsical impulse that prompted them both, and was born, no doubt, of the circumstance and mood of that first evening, they did not seek to learn more. They feared—though they did not say it—that to learn the identity of the musician would rob them of the peculiar pleasure they found in the music, itself. So they spoke always of their unknown neighbor in a fanciful vein, as in like humor they spoke of the spirit that Aaron King still insisted haunted the place, or as they alluded to the mystery of the carefully tended rose garden.

When the artist could put it off no longer, a day was finally set when Mrs. Taine was to come for the beginning of her portrait. The appointed hour found the artist in his studio. A canvas stood ready upon the easel; palette, colors and brushes were at hand. The painter was standing at the big, north window, looking up away to the mountains—the mountains that the novelist said called so insistently. Suddenly, he turned his head to listen. Sweetly clear and low, through the green wall of the orange-trees, came the music of that hidden violin.

As he stood there,—with his eyes fixed upon the mountains, listening to the spirit that spoke in the tones of the unseen instrument,—Aaron King knew, all at once, that the passing moment was one of those rare moments—that come, all unexpectedly—when, with prophetic vision, one sees clearly the end of the course he pursues and the destiny that waits him at its completion. As clearly, too, he saw the other way, and knew the meaning of the vision. But seldom is the strength given to man, in such moments, to choose for himself. Though he may see the other way clearly, his feet cling to the path he has elected to follow; nor will he, unless some one takes him by the hand saying, "Come," turn aside.

A voice, not at all in harmony with the music, broke upon the artist's consciousness. He turned to see Mrs. Taine standing expectantly in the open door. "Hush!" said the painter, still under the spell of that moment so big with possibilities. "Listen,"—with a gesture, he checked her advance,—"listen."

A look of haughty surprise flashed over the woman's too perfect features. Then, as her ear caught the tones of the violin, she half turned—but only for a moment.

"Very clever, isn't it," she said as she came forward "It must be old Professor Becker. He lives somewhere around here, I understand. They say he is very good."

The artist looked at her for an instant, in amazement Then, as his normal mind asserted itself, he burst into an embarrassed laugh.

At her look of puzzled inquiry, he said, "I beg your pardon, Mrs. Taine. I did not realize how harshly I greeted you. The fact is I—I was dreaming"—he turned suggestively toward the canvas upon the easel. "You see I was expecting you—I was thinking—then the music came—and—well—when you actually appeared in the flesh, I did not for the moment realize that it was really you."

"How charming of you!" she returned. "To be made the subject of an artist's dream—really it is quite the nicest compliment I have ever received. Tell me, do you like me in this?" she slipped the wrap she wore from her shoulders, and stood before him, gowned in the simple, gray dress of a Quaker Maid. Deliberately, she turned her beautiful self about for his critical inspection. Moving to and fro, sitting, half-reclining, standing—in various graceful poses she invited, challenged, dared, his closest attention— professional attention, of course—to every curve and detail.

In spite of its simplicity of color and line, the gown still bore the unmistakable stamp of the wearer's world. The severity of line was subtly made to emphasize the voluptuousness of the body that was covered but not hidden. The quiet color was made to accentuate the flesh the dress concealed only to reveal. The very lack of ornament but served to center the attention upon the charms that so loudly professed to scorn them. It was worldliness speaking in the quiet voice of religion. It was vulgarity advertising itself in terms of good taste. She had made modesty the handmaiden of blatant immodesty, and the daring impudence of it all fairly stunned the painter.

"Oh dear!" she said, watching his face, "I fear you don't like it, at all—and I thought it such a beautiful little gown. You told me to wear whatever I pleased, you know."

"It is a beautiful gown," he said—then added impulsively, "and you are beautiful in it. You would be beautiful in anything."

She shook her head; favoring him with an understanding smile. "You say that to please me. I can see that you don't like me this way."

"But I do," he insisted. "I like you that way, immensely. I was a bit surprised, that's all. You see, I thought, of course, that you would select an evening gown of some sort—something, you know, that would fit your social position—your place in the world. In this costume, the beauty of your shoulders—"

Lowering her eyes as if embarrassed, she said coldly, "The beauty of my shoulders is not for the public. I have never worn—I will not wear—one of those dreadful, immodest gowns."

Aaron King was bewildered. Suddenly, he remembered what Conrad Lagrange had said about her fad. But after so frankly exhibiting herself before him, dressed as she was in a gown that was deliberately planned to advertise her physical charms, to be particular about baring her shoulders in a conventional costume—! It was quite too much.

"Again, I beg your pardon, Mrs. Taine," he managed to say. "I did not know. Under the circumstances, this is exactly the thing. Your portrait, in what is so frankly a costume assumed for the purpose, takes us out of the dilemma very nicely, indeed."

"Why, that's exactly what I thought," she returned eagerly. "And this is so in keeping with my real tastes—don't you see? A real portrait—I mean a serious work of art, you know—should always be something more than a mere likeness, should it not? Don't you think that to be genuinely good, a portrait must reveal the spirit and character—must portray the soul, as well as the features? I do so want this to be a truly great picture—for your sake." Her manner seemed to say that she was doing it all for him. "I have never permitted any one to paint my portrait before, you know," she added meaningly.

"You are very kind, Mrs. Taine," he returned gravely. "Believe me, I do appreciate this opportunity I shall do my best to express my appreciation here"—he indicated the canvas on the easel.

When his sitter was posed to his liking, and the artist, with a few bold, sweeping, strokes of the charcoal had roughed out his subject on the canvas, and was bending over his color-box—he said, casually, to put her at ease, "You came alone this afternoon, did you?"

"Oh, no, indeed! I brought Louise with me. I shall always bring her, or some one. One cannot be too careful, you know," she added with simulated artlessness.

The painter, studying her face, replied mechanically "No indeed."

As he turned back to his canvas, Mrs. Taine continued, "I left her in the house, with a box of chocolates and a novel. I felt that you would rather we were alone."

"Please don't look down," said the artist. "I want your eyes about here"—he indicated a picture on the wall, a little back and to the left of where he stood at the easel.

After this, there was silence in the studio, for a little while. Mrs. Taine obediently kept the pose; her eyes upon the point the artist had indicated; but—as the man, himself, was almost directly in her line of vision—it was easy for her to watch him at his work, when his eyes were on his canvas or palette. The arrangement was admirable in that it relieved the tedium of the hour for the sitter; and gave her face an expression of animated interest that, truthfully fixed upon the canvas, should insure the fame and future of any painter.

It would be quite too much to say that Aaron King became absorbed in his occupation. Thorough master of the tools of his craft, and of his own technic, as well; he was interested in the mere exercising of his skill, but he in no sense lost himself in his work. Two or three times, Mrs. Taine saw him glance quickly over his shoulder, as though expecting some one. Once, for quite a moment, he deliberately turned from his easel to stand at the window, looking up at the distant mountain peaks. Several times, he seemed to be listening.

"May I talk?" she said at last.

"Why, certainly," he returned. "I want you to feel perfectly at ease. You must be altogether at home here. Just let yourself go—say what you like, with no conventional restraints whatever—consider me a mechanical something that is no more than an article of furniture—be as thoroughly yourself as if alone in your own room."

"How funny," she said musingly.

"Not at all"—he returned—"just a matter of business."

"But it would be funny if I were to take you at your word," she replied; suddenly breaking the pose and meeting his gaze squarely. "Is it—is it quite necessary for the mechanical something to look at me like that?"

"I said that you were to consider me as an article of furniture. I didn't say that I felt like a table or chair."

"Oh!"

"Don't look down; keep the pose, please," came somewhat sharply from the man at the easel, as though he were mentally taking himself in hand.

After that, she watched him with increasing interest and, when he turned his head in that listening attitude, a curious, resentful light came into her eyes.

Presently, she asked abruptly, "What is it that you hear?"

"I thought I heard music," he answered, coloring slightly and turning to his work with suddenly absorbing interest.

"The violin that so enchanted you when I came to break the spell?" she persisted playfully—though the light in her eyes was not a playful light.

"Yes," he answered shortly; stepping back and shading his eyes with his hand for a careful look at his canvas.

"And don't you know who it is?"

"You said it was an old professor somebody."

"That was my first guess," she retorted. "Was I right?"

"I don't know."

"But it comes from that little box of a house, next door, doesn't it?"

"Evidently," the artist answered. Then, laying aside his palette and brushes he said abruptly, "That is all for to-day; thank you."

"Oh, so soon!" she exclaimed; and the regret in her voice was very pleasing to the man who was decidedly not a mechanical something.

She started eagerly forward toward the easel. But the artist, with a quick motion, drew a curtain across the canvas, to hide his work; while he checked her with—"Not yet, please. I don't want you to see it until I say you may."

"How mean of you," she protested; charmingly submissive. Then, eagerly—"And do you want me to-morrow? You do, don't you?"

"Yes, please—at the same hour."

When the Quaker Maiden's dress was safely hidden under her wrap, Mrs. Taine stood, for a moment, looking thoughtfully about the studio; while the artist waited at the door, ready to escort her to the automobile. "I am going to love this room," she said slowly; and, for the first time, her voice was genuinely sincere, with a hint of wistfulness in its tone that made him regard her wonderingly.

She went to him impulsively. "Will you, when you are famous—when you are a great artist and all the great and famous people go to you to have their portraits painted—will you remember poor me, I wonder?"

"Am I really going to be famous?" he returned doubtfully. "Are you so sure that this picture will mean success?"

"Of course I am sure—I know. You want to succeed don't you?"

Aaron King returned her look, for a moment, without answering. Then, with a quick, fierce determination that betrayed a depth of feeling she had never before seen in him, he exclaimed, "Do I want to succeed! I—I must succeed. I tell you I must."

And the woman answered very softly, with her hand upon his arm, "And you shall—you shall."

Conrad Lagrange and Czar found the artist on the front porch, pulling moodily at his pipe.

"Is it all over for to-day?" asked the novelist as he stood looking down upon the young man with that peculiarly piercing, baffling gaze.

"All over," replied the artist, answering the greeting thrust of Czar's muzzle against his knee, with caressing hand. "Where did you fly to?"

The other dropped into a chair. "I would fly anywhere to escape being entertained by that Ragtime' piece of human nonentity—Louise Taine. I saw them coming, just in time." He was filling his pipe as he spoke. "And how did the work go?"

"All right," replied the painter, indifferently.

The older man shot a curious sidewise glance at his moody companion; then, striking a match, he gave careful attention to his pipe. Watching the cloud of blue smoke, he said quizzingly, "I suppose 'Her Majesty' was royally apparelled for the occasion-properly arrayed in purple and fine linen; as befits the dignity of her state?"

The artist turned at the mocking, suggestive tone and answered savagely, "I suppose you have got to know, damn you! I'm painting her as a Quaker Maiden."

Conrad Lagrange's reply was as surprising in its way as was the outburst of the artist. Instead of the tirade of biting sarcasm and stinging abuse that the painter expected, the older man only gazed at him from under his scowling brows and, shaking his head, sadly, said with sincere regret and understanding "You poor fellow! It must be hell." Then, as his keen mind grasped the full significance of the artist's words, he murmured meditatively, "The personification of the age masquerading in Quaker gray—Shades of the giants who used to be! What an opportunity—if you only had the nerve to do it."

The artist flung out his hand in protest as he rose from his chair to pace up and down the porch. "Don't, Lagrange, don't! I can't stand it, just now."

"All right." said the other, heartily, "I won't." Rising, he put his hand on his friend's shoulder. "Come, let's go for a look at the roses, before Yee Kee calls us to dinner."

In the garden, the artist's eye caught sight of something white lying in the well-kept path. With an exclamation, he went quickly to pick it up. It was a dainty square of lace—a handkerchief—with an exquisitely embroidered "S" in the corner.

The two men looked at each other in silence; with smiling, questioning eyes.

Chapter VIII

The Portrait That Was Not a Portrait

Aaron King was putting the last touches to his portrait of the woman who—Conrad Lagrange said—was the personification of the age.

From that evening when the young man told his friend the story of his mother's sacrifice, their friendship had become like that friendship which passeth the love of women. While the novelist, true to his promise, did not cease to flay his younger companion—for the good of the artist's soul—those moments when his gentler moods ruled his speech were, perhaps, more frequent; and the artist was more and more learning to appreciate the rare imagination, the delicacy of feeling, the intellectual brilliancy, and the keenness of mental vision that distinguished the man whose life was so embittered by the use he had made of his own rich gifts.

The novelist steadily refused to look at the picture while the work was in progress. He said, bluntly, that he preferred to run no risk of interfering with the young man's chance for fame; and that it would be quite enough for him to look upon his friend's shame when it was accomplished; without witnessing the process in its various stages. The artist laughed to hide the embarrassing fact that he was rather pleased to be left to himself with this particular picture.

Conrad Lagrange did not, however, refuse to accompany his friend, occasionally, to the house on Fairlands Heights; where the painter continued to spend much of his time. When Mrs. Taine made mocking references to the novelist's promise not to leave the artist unprotected to her tender mercies, he always answered with some—as she said—twisty saying; to the effect that the present situation in no way lessened his determination to save the young man from the influences that would accomplish the ruin of his genius. "If"—he always added—"if he is worth saving; which remains to be seen." Always, at the Taine home, they met James Rutlidge. Frequently the celebrated critic dropped in at the cottage in the orange grove.

Under the skillful management of Rutlidge,—at the request of Mrs. Taine,—the newspapers were already busy with the name and work of Aaron King. True, the critic had never seen the artist's work; but, never-the-less, the papers and magazines throughout the country often mentioned the high order of the painter's genius. There were little stories of his study and success abroad; tactful references to his aristocratic family; entertaining accounts of his romantic life with the famous novelist in the orange groves of Fairlands, and of how, in his California studio among the roses, the distinguished painter was at work upon a portrait of the well-known social leader, Mrs. Taine—this being the first portrait ever painted of that famous beauty. That the picture would create a sensation at the exhibition, was the unanimous verdict of all who had been permitted to see the marvelous creation by this rare genius whose work was so little known in this country.

Said Conrad Lagrange—"It is all so easy."

Once or twice, the artist or his friend had seen the woman of the disfigured face; and the novelist still tried in vain to fix her in his memory. Every day, they heard, in the depths of the neighboring orange grove, the music of that unseen violin. They spoke, often, in playful mood, of the spirit that haunted the place; but they made no effort to solve the mystery of the carefully tended rose garden. They knew that whoever cared for the roses worked there only in the early morning hours; and they carefully avoided going into the yard back of the house until after breakfast. They felt that an investigation might rob them of the peculiar humor of their fancy—a fancy that was to them, both, such a pleasure; and gave to their home amid the orange-trees and roses such an added charm.

But the other member of the trio of friends was not so reticent. Czar had formed an—to his most proper dogship—unusual habit. Frequently, when the three were sitting on the porch in the evening, he would rise suddenly from his place beside his master's chair, and walking sedately to the side of the porch facing that neighboring gable and chimney, would stand listening attentively; then, without so much as a "by-your-leave," he would leap to the ground, and vanish somewhere around the corner of the house. Later, he would come sedately back; greeting each, in turn, with that insistent thrust his soft muzzle against a knee; and assuring them, in the wordless speech of his expressive, brown eyes, that his mission had been a most proper one, and that they might trust him to make no foolish mistakes that would mar the peace and harmony of their little household. The men never failed to agree with him that it was all right. In fact, so fully did they trust him that they never even stepped to the corner of the porch to see where he went; nor would they leave their chairs until he had returned.

Upon those days when Mrs. Taine came to the studio,—being always careful that Louise accompanied her as far as the house,—Conrad Lagrange vanished. The man swore by all the strange and wonderful gods he knew—and they were many—that he feared to spend an hour with that effervescing young female devotee of the Arts—lest the mountains in their wrath should fall upon him.

But that day, when Mrs. Taine came for the last sitting, the novelist—engaged in interesting talk with the artist—forgot.

"You are caught," cried the painter, gleefully, as the big automobile stopped at the gate.

"I'll be damned if I am," retorted the novelist, with no profane intent but with meaning quite literal; and, seizing a book, he bolted through the kitchen—nearly upsetting the startled Yee Kee.

"What's matte'," inquired the Chinaman, putting his head in at the living-room door; his almond eyes as wide as they could go, with an expression of celestial consternation that convulsed the artist. Catching sight of the automobile, his oriental features wrinkled into a yellow grin of understanding; "Oh! see um come! Ha! I know. He all time go, she come. He say no like lagtime gal. Dog Cza', him all time gone, too; him no like lagtime—all same Miste' Laglange. Ha! I go, too," and he, in turn, vanished.

"You are early, to-day," said Aaron King, as he escorted Mrs. Taine to the studio.

Just inside the door, she turned impulsively to face him—standing close, her beautifully groomed and voluptuous body instinct with the lure of her sex, her too perfect features slightly flushed, and her eyes submissively downcast. "And have you forgotten that this is the last time I can come?" she asked in a low tone.

"Surely not"—he returned calmly—"you are coming to-morrow, with the others, aren't you?" Her husband with James Rutlidge and Louise Taine were invited for the next day, to view the portrait.

"Oh, but that will be so different!" She loosed the wrap she wore, and threw it aside with an indescribable familiar gesture. "You don't realize what these hours have meant to me—how could you? You do not live in my world. Your world is—is so different You do not know—you do not know." With a sudden burst of passion, she added, "The world that I live in is hell; and this—this—oh, it has been heavenly!"

Her words, her voice, the poise of her figure, the gesture with outstretched arms—it was all so nearly an invitation, so nearly a surrender of herself to him, that the man started forward impulsively. For the moment he forgot his work—he forgot everything—he was conscious only of the woman who stood before him. But even as the light of triumph blazed up in the woman's eyes, the man halted,—drew back; and his face was turned from her as he listened to the sweetly appealing message of the gentle spirit that made itself felt in the music of that hidden violin. It was as though, in truth, the mountains, themselves,—from their calm heights so remote from the little world wherein men live their baser tragedies,—watched over him. "Don't you think we had better proceed with our work?" he said calmly.

The light in the woman's eyes changed to anger which she turned away to hide. Without replying, she went to her place and assumed the pose; and, as she had watched him day after day when his eyes were upon the canvas, she watched him now. Since that first day, when she had questioned him about the unseen musician, they had not mentioned the subject, although—as was inevitable under the circumstances—their intimacy had grown. But not once had he turned from his work in that listening attitude, or looked from the window as though half-expecting some one, without her noting it. And, always, her eyes had flashed with resentment, which she had promptly concealed when the painter, again turning to his easel, had looked from his canvas to her face.

Scarcely was the artist well started in his work, that afternoon, when the music ceased. Presently, Mrs. Taine broke her watchful silence, with the quite casual remark; "Your musical neighbor is still unknown to you, I suppose?"

"Yes,"—he answered smiling, as though more to himself than at her,—"we have never tried to make her acquaintance."

The woman caught him up quickly; "To make her acquaintance? Why do you say, 'her,' if you do not know who it is?"

The artist was confused. "Did I say, her?" he questioned, his face flushed with embarrassment. "It was a slip of the tongue. Neither Conrad Lagrange nor I know anything about our neighbor."

She laughed ironically. "And you could know so easily."

"I suppose so; but we have never cared to. We prefer to accept the music as it comes to us—impersonally—for what it is—not for whoever makes it." He spoke coldly, as though the subject was distasteful to him, under the circumstances of the moment.

But the woman persisted. "Well, I know who it is. Shall I tell you?"

"No. I do not care to know. I am not interested in the musician."

"Oh, but you might be, you know," she retorted.

"Please take the pose," returned Aaron King professionally. Mrs. Taine, wisely, for the time, dropped the subject; contenting herself with a meaning laugh.

The artist silently gave all his attention to the nearly finished portrait. He was not painting, now, with full brush and swift sure strokes,—as had been his way when building up his picture,—but worked with occasional deft touches here and there; drawing back from the canvas often, to study it intently, his eyes glancing swiftly from the picture to the sitter's face and back again to the portrait; then stepping forward quickly, ready brush in hand; to withdraw an instant later for another long and searching study. Presently, with an air of relief, he laid aside his palette and brushes; and turning to Mrs. Taine, with a smile, held out his hand. "Come," he said, "tell me if I have done well or ill."

"It is finished?" she cried. "I may see it?"

"It is all that I can do"—he answered—"come." He led her to the easel, where they stood side by side before his work.

The picture, still fresh from the painter's brush, was a portrait of Mrs. Taine—yet not a portrait. Exquisite in coloring and in its harmony of tone and line, it betrayed in every careful detail—in every mark of the brush—the thoughtful, painstaking care—the thorough knowledge and highly trained skill of an artist who was, at least, master of his own technic. But—if one might say so—the painting was more a picture than a portrait. The face upon the canvas was the face of Mrs. Taine, indeed, in that the features were her features; but it was also the face of a sweetly modest Quaker Maid. The too perfect, too well cared for face of the beautiful woman of the world was, on the canvas, given the charm of a natural unconscious loveliness. The eyes that had watched the artist with such certain knowledge of life and with the boldness born of that knowledge were, in the picture, beautiful with the charm of innocent maidenhood. The very coloring and the arrangement of the hair were changed subtly to express, not the skill of high-priced beauty-doctors and of fashionable hair-dressers, but the instinctive care of womanliness. The costume that, when worn by the woman, expressed so fully her true character; in the picture, became the emblem of a pure and deeply religious spirit.

Mrs. Taine turned impulsively to the artist, and, placing her hand upon his arm, exclaimed in delight, "Oh, is it true? Am I really so beautiful?"

The artist laughed. "You like it?"

"Like it? How could I help liking it? It is lovely."

"I am glad," he returned. "I hoped it would please you."

"And you"—she asked, with eager eyes—"are you satisfied with it? Does it seem good to you?"

"Oh, as for that," he answered, "I suppose one is never satisfied. I know the work is good—in a way. But it is very far from what it should be, I fear. I feel that, after all, I have not made the most of my opportunity." He spoke with a shade of sadness.

Again, she put out her hand impulsively to touch his arm, as she answered eagerly, "Ah, but no one else will say that. No one else will dare. It will be the sensation of the year—I tell you. Just you wait until Jim Rutlidge sees it. Wait until it is hung for exhibition, and he tells the world about it. Everybody worth while will be coming to you then. And I—I will remember these hours with you, and be glad that I could help—even so little. Will you remember them, too, I wonder. Are you glad the picture is finished?"

"And are you not glad?" he returned meaningly.

They had both forgotten the painting before them. They did not see it. They each saw only the other.

"No, I am not glad," she said in a low tone. "People would very soon be talking if I should come here, alone—now that the picture is finished."

"I suppose in any case you will be leaving Fairlands soon, for the summer," he returned slowly.

"O listen,"—she cried with quick eagerness—"we are going to Lake Silence. What's to hinder your coming too? Everybody goes there, you know. Won't you come?"

"But would it be altogether safe?" He reflected doubtfully.

"Why, of course,—Mr. Taine, Louise, and Jim,—we are all going together—don't you see? I don't believe you want to go," she pouted. "I believe you want to forget."

Her alluring manner, the invitation conveyed in her words and voice, the touch of her hand on his arm, and the nearness of her person, fairly swept the man off his feet. With quick passion, he caught her hand, and his words came with reckless heat. "You know that I will not forget you. You know that I could not, if I would. Do you think that I have been so engrossed with my brushes and canvas that I have been unconscious of you? What is that painted thing beside your own beautiful self? Do you think that because I must turn myself into a machine to make a photograph of your beauty, I am insensible to its charm? I am not a machine. I am a man; as you are a woman; and I—"

She checked him suddenly—stepping aside with a quick movement, and the words, "Hush, some one is coming."

The artist, too, heard voices, just without the door.

Mrs. Taine moved swiftly across the room toward her wrap. Aaron King, going to his easel, drew the velvet curtain to hide the picture.

Chapter IX

Conrad Lagrange's Adventure

Certainly, when Conrad Lagrange fled so precipitately from Louise Taine, that afternoon, he had no thought that the trivial incident was to mark the beginning of a new era in his life; or that it would work out in the life of his dearest friend such far reaching results. His only purpose was to escape an hour of the frothy vaporings of the poor, young creature who believed herself so interested in art and letters, and who succeeded so admirably in expressing the spirit of her environment and training.

With his pipe and book, the novelist hid himself in the rose garden; finding a seat on the ground, in an angle of the studio wall and the Ragged Robin hedge, where any one entering the enclosure would be least likely to observe him. Czar, heartily approving of his master's action, stretched himself comfortably under the nearest rose-bush, and waited further developments.

Presently, the novelist heard his friend, with Mrs. Taine, come from the house and enter the studio. For a moment, he entertained the uncomfortable fear that the artist, in a spirit of sheer boyish fun that so often moved him, would bring Mrs. Taine to the garden. But the moment passed, and the novelist,—mentally blessing the young man for his forbearance,—with a chuckle of satisfaction, lighted his pipe and opened his book. Scarcely had he found his place in the pages, however, when he was again interrupted—this time, by the welcome tones of their neighbor's violin. Putting his book aside, the man reclining in the shelter of the roses, with half-closed eyes, yielded himself to the fancy of the spirit that called from the depths of the fragrant orange grove.

The mass of roses in the hedge and on the wall of the studio above his head dropped their lovely petals down upon him. The warm, slanting rays of the afternoon sun, softened by the screen of shining leaves and branches, played over the bewildering riot of color. Here and there, golden-bodied bees and velvet-winged butterflies flitted about their fairy-like duties. Far above, in the deep blue, a hawk floated on motionless wings and a lonely crow laid his course toward the distant mountain peaks that gleamed, silvery white, above the blue and purple of the lower ridges and the tawny yellow of their foothills. The air was saturated with the fragrance of the rose and orange blossoms, of eucalyptus and pepper trees, and with the thousand other perfumes of a California spring.

The music ceased. The man waited—hoping that it would begin again. But it did not; and he was about to take up his book, once more, when Czar arose, stretched himself, stood for a moment in a picturesque, listening attitude, then trotted off among the roses; leaving the novelist with an odd feeling of uneasy expectancy—half resolved to stay, half determined to go. The thought of Louise in the house decided him, and he kept his place, hidden as he was, in the corner—a whimsical smile hovering over his world-lined features as though, after all, he felt himself entering upon some enjoyable adventure.

Presently, he heard indistinctly, somewhere in the other end of the garden, a low murmuring voice. As it came nearer, the man's smile grew more pronounced It was a wonderfully attractive voice, clear and full in its pure-toned sweetness. The unseen speaker was talking to the novelist's dog. The smile on the man's face was still more pronounced, as he whispered to himself, "The rascal! So this is what he has been up to!" Rising quietly to his knees, he peered through the flower-laden bushes.

A young woman of rare and exquisite beauty was moving about the garden—bending over the roses, and talking in low tones to Czar, who—to his hidden master—appeared to appreciate fully the favor of his gentle companion's intimacy. The novelist—old in the study of character and trained by his long years of observation and experience in the world of artificiality—was fascinated by the loveliness of the scene.

Dressed simply, in some soft clinging material of white, with a modestly low-cut square at the throat, and sleeves that ended in filmy lace just below the elbow—her lithe, softly rounded form, as she moved here and there, had all the charm of girlish grace with the fuller beauty of ripening womanhood. As she bent over the roses, or stooped to caress the dog, in gentle comradeship, her step, her poise, her every motion, was instinct with that strength and health that is seldom seen among those who wear the shackles of a too conventionalized society. Her face,—warmly tinted by the golden out-of-doors, firm fleshed and clear,—in its unconscious naturalness and in its winsome purity was like the flowers she stooped to kiss.

As he watched, the man noticed—with a smile of understanding—that she kept rather to the side of the garden toward the house; where the artist, at his easel by the big, north light, could not see her through the small window in the end of the room; and where, hidden by the tall hedge, she would not be noticed from Yee Kee's kitchen. Often, too, she paused to listen, as if for any chance approaching step— appearing, to the fancy of the man, as some creature from another world—poised lightly, ready to vanish if any rude observer came too near. Soon,—after a cautious, hesitating, listening look about,— she slipped, swift footed as a fawn, across the garden, and—followed by the dog—disappeared into the latticed rose-covered arbor against the southern wall.

With a chuckle to himself, Conrad Lagrange crept quietly along the hedge to the door of her retreat.

When she saw him there, she gave a little cry and started as though to escape. But the novelist, smiling barred her way; while Czar, joyfully greeting his master, turned from the man to the girl and back to the man again, as if, by dividing his attention equally between the two, he was bent upon assuring each that the other was a friend of the right sort. There was no mistaking the facts that the dog was introducing them, and that he was as proud of his new acquaintance as he was pleased to present his older and more intimate companion.

A sunny smile broke over the girl's winsome face, as she caught the meaning of Czar's behavior. "O," she said, "are you his master?" Her manner was as natural and unrestrained as a child's—her voice, musically sweet and low, as one unaccustomed to the speech of noisy, crowded cities or shrill chattering crowds.

"I am his most faithful and humble subject," returned the man, whimsically.

She was studying his face openly, while her own countenance—unschooled to hide emotions, untrained to deceive—frankly betrayed each passing thought and mood. The daintily turned chin, sensitive lips, delicate nostrils, and large, blue eyes,—with that wide, unafraid look of a child that has never been taught to fear,—revealed a spirit fine and rare; while the low, broad forehead, shaded by a wealth of soft brown hair,—that, arranged deftly in some simple fashion, seemed to invite the caress of every wayward breath of air,—gave the added charm of strength and purpose. The man, seeing these things and knowing—as few men ever know—their value, waited her verdict.

It came with a smile and a pretty fancy, as though she caught the mood of the novelist's reply. "He has told me so much about you—how kind you are to him, and how he loves you. I hope you don't mind that he and I have learned to be good friends. Won't you tell me his name? I have tried everything, but nothing seems to fit. To call such a royal fellow, 'doggie', doesn't do at all, does it?"

Conrad Lagrange laughed—and it was the laugh of a Conrad Lagrange unknown to the world. "No," he said with mock seriousness, "'doggie,' doesn't do at all. He's not that kind of a dog. His name is Czar. That is"—he added, giving full rein to his droll humor—"I gave it to him for a name. He has made it his title. He did that, you know, so I would always remember that he is my superior."

She laughed—low, full-throated and clear—as a girl who has not sadly learned that she is a woman, laughs. Then she fell to caressing the dog and calling him by name; while Czar—in his efforts to express his delight and satisfaction—was as nearly undignified as it was possible for him to be.

As he watched them, the rugged, world-worn features of the famous novelist were lighted with an expression that transformed them.

"And I suppose," she said,—still responding to the novelist's playful mood,—"that Czar told you I was trespassing in your garden. Of course it was his duty to tell. I hope he told you, also, that I do not steal your roses."

The man shook his head, and his sharp, green-gray eyes were twinkling merrily, now—as a boy in the spirit of some amusing venture. "Oh, no! Czar said nothing at all about trespassers. He did tell me, though, about a wonderful creature that comes every day to visit the garden. A nymph, he thought it was—a beautiful Oread from away up there among the silver peaks and purple canyons—or, perhaps, a lovely Dryad from among the oaks and pines. I felt quite sure, though, that the nymph must be an Oread; because he said that she comes to gather colors from the roses, and that every morning and every evening she uses these colors to tint the highest peaks and crests of her mountains—making them so beautiful that mortals would always begin and end each day by looking up at them. Of course, the moment I saw, you I knew who you were."

Unaffectedly pleased as a child at his quaint fancy, she answered merrily, "And so you hid among the roses to trap me, I suppose."

"Indeed, I did not," he retorted indignantly. "I was forced to fly from a wicked Flibbertigibbet who seeks to torment me. I barely escaped with my life, and came into the garden to hide and recover from my fright. Then I heard the most wonderful music and guessed that you must be somewhere around. Then Czar, who had come with me to hide from the Flibbertigibbet in the house, left me. I looked to see where he had gone, and so I saw, sure enough, that it was you. All my life, you know, I have wanted to catch a real nymph; but never could. So when you came into the arbor, I couldn't resist trying again. And, now, here we are—with Czar to say it is all right."

At his fanciful words, she laughed again, and her cheeks flushed with pleasure. Then, with grave sweetness, she said, "Won't you sit down, please, and let me explain seriously?"

"I suppose you must pretend to be like the rest of us," he returned with an air of resignation, "but all the same, Czar and I know you are not."

When they were seated, she said simply, "My name is Sibyl Andres. This place used to be my home. My mother planted this garden with her own hands. Many of these roses were brought from our home in the mountains, where I was born, and where I lived with father and mother until five years ago. I feel, still, as though the old place in the hills were my real home, and every summer, when nearly every one goes away from Fairlands and there is nothing for me to do, Myra Willard and I go up there, for as long as we can. You see, I teach music and play in the churches. Miss Willard taught me. She and mother are the only teachers I have ever had. After father's death, mother and Myra and I lived here for two years; then mother died, and Myra and I moved to that little house over there, because we could not afford to keep this place. But the man who bought it gave me permission to care for the garden; so I come almost every day—through that little gate in the corner of the hedge, there—to tend the roses. Since you men moved in, though, I come, mostly, in the morning—early—before you are up. I only slip in, sometimes, for a few minutes, in the afternoon—when I think it will be safe. You see, being strangers, I—I feared you would think me bold—if I—if I asked to come. So many people really wouldn't understand, you know."

Conrad Lagrange's deep voice was very gentle as he said, "Mr. King and I have known, all the time, that we had no real claim upon this garden, Miss Andrés." Then, with his whimsical smile, he added, "You see, we felt, from the very first, that it was haunted by a lovely spirit that would vanish utterly if we intruded. That is why we have been so careful. We did not want to frighten you away. And besides, you know, Czar told us that it was all right!"

The blue eyes shone through a bright mist as she answered the man's kindly words. "You are good, Mr. Lagrange. And all the time it was really you of whom I was so afraid."

"Why me, more than my friend?" he asked, regarding her thoughtfully.

She colored a little under his searching gaze, but answered with that childlike frankness that was so much a part of her winsome charm, "Why, because your friend is an artist—I thought he would be sure to understand. I knew, of course, that you were the famous author; everybody talks about your living here." She seemed to think that her words explained.

"You mean that you were afraid of me because I am famous?" he asked doubtfully.

"Oh no," she answered, "not because you are famous. I mean—I was not afraid of your fame," she smiled.

"And now," said the novelist decisively, "you must tell me at once—do you read my books?" He waited, as though much depended upon her answer.

The blue eyes were gazing at him with that wide, unafraid look as she answered sadly, "No, sir. I have tried, but I can't. They spoil my music. They hurt me, somehow, all over."

Conrad Lagrange received her words with mingled emotions—with pleased delight at her ingenuous frankness; with bitter shame, sorrow, and humiliation and, at the last, with genuine gladness and relief. "I knew it"—he said triumphantly—"I knew it. It was because of my books that you were so afraid of me?" He asked eagerly, as one would ask to have a deep conviction verified.

"You see," she said,—smiling at the manner of his words,—"I did not know that an author could be so different from the things he writes about." Then, with a puzzled air—"But why do you write the horrid things that spoil my music and make me afraid? Why don't you write as you talk—about—about the mountains? Why don't you make books like—like"—she seemed to be searching for a word, and smiled with pleasure when she found it—"like yourself?"

"Listen"—said the novelist impressively, taking refuge in his fanciful humor—"listen—I'll tell you a secret that must always be for just you and me—you like secrets don't you?"—anxiously.

She laughed with pleasure—responding instantly to his mood. "Of course I like secrets."

He nodded approval. "I was sure you did. Now listen—I am not really Conrad Lagrange, the man who wrote those books that hurt you so—not when I am here in your rose garden, or when I am listening to your music, or when I am away up there in your mountains, you know. It is only when I am in the unclean world that reads and likes my books that I am the man who wrote them."

Her eyes shone with quick understanding. "Of course," she agreed, "you couldn't be that kind of a man, and love the music, and like to be here among the roses or up in the mountains, could you?"

"No, and I'll tell you something else that goes with our secret. Your name is not really Sibyl Andrés, you know—any more than you really live over there in that little house. Your real home is in the mountains—just as you said—you really live among the glowing peaks, under the dark pines, on the ridges, and in the purple shadows of the canyons. You only come down here to the Fairlands folk with a message from your mountains—and we call your message music. Your name is—"

She was leaning forward, her face glowing with eagerness. "What is my name?"

"What can it be but 'Nature'," he said softly. "That's it, 'Nature'."

"And you? Who are you when you are not—when you are not in that other world?"

"Me? Oh, my real name is 'Civilization'. Can't you guess why?"

She shook her head. "Tell me."

"Because,—in spite of all that the world that reads my books can give,—poor old 'Civilization' cannot be happy without the message that 'Nature' brings from her mountains."

"And you, too, love the mountains and—and this garden, and my music?" she asked half doubtingly. "You are not pretending that too—just to amuse me?"

"No, I am not pretending that," he said.

"Then why—how can you do the—the other thing? I can't understand."

"Of course, you can't understand—how could you? You are 'Nature' and 'Nature' must often be puzzled by the things that 'Civilization' does."

"Yes. I think that is true," she agreed. "But I'm glad you like my music, anyway."

"And so am I glad—that I can like it. That's the only thing that saves me."

"And your friend, the artist,—does he like my mountain music, do you think?"

"Very much. He needs it too."

"I am glad," she answered simply. "I hoped he would like it, and that it would help him. It was really for him that I have played."

"You played for him?"

"Yes," she returned without confusion. "You see, I did not know about you—then. I thought you were altogether the man who wrote those books—and so I could not play for you. That is—I mean—you understand—I could not play—" again she seemed to search for a word, and finding it, smiled—"I could not play myself for you. But I thought that because he was an artist he would understand; and that if I could make the music tell him of the mountains it would, perhaps, help him a little to make his work beautiful and right—do you see?"

"Yes," he answered smilingly, "I see. I might have known that it was for him that you brought your message from the hills. But poor old 'Civilization' is frightfully stupid sometimes, you know."

Laughingly, she turned to the lattice wall of the arbor, and parting the screen of vines a little, said to him, "Look here!"

Standing beside her, Conrad Lagrange, through the window in the end of the studio next the garden, saw Aaron King at his easel; the artist's position in the light of the big, north window being in a direct line between the two openings and the arbor. Mrs. Taine was sitting too far out of line to be seen.

The girl laughed gleefully. "Do you see him at his work? At first, I only hid here to find what kind of people were going to live in my old home. But when he was making our old barn into a studio, and I heard who you both were, I came because I love to watch him; as I try to make the music I think he would love to hear."

The novelist studied her intently. She was so artless—so unaffected by the conventions of the world—in a word, so natural in expressing her thoughts, that the man who had given the best years of his life to feed the vicious, grossly sensual and bestial imaginations of his readers was deeply moved. He was puzzled what to say. At last, he murmured haltingly, "You like the artist, then?"

Her eyes were full of curious laughter as she answered, "Why, what a funny question—when I have never even talked with him. How could I like any one I have never known?"

"But you make your music for him; and you come here to watch him?"

"Oh, but that is for the work he is doing; that is for his pictures." She turned to look through the tiny opening in the arbor. "How I wish I could see inside that beautiful room. I know it must be beautiful. Once, when you were all gone, I tried to steal in; but, of course, he keeps it locked."

"I'll tell you what we'll do," said the man, suddenly—prompted by her confession to resume his playful mood.

"What?" she asked eagerly, in a like spirit of fun.

"First," he answered, half teasingly, "I must know if you could, now, make your music for me as well as for him."

"For the you that loves the mountains and the garden I'm sure I could," she answered promptly.

"Well then, if you will promise to do that—if you will promise not to play yourself for just him alone but for me too—I'll fix it so that you can go into the studio yonder."

"Oh, I will always play for you, too, anyway—now that I know you."

"Of course," he said, "we could just walk up to the door, and I could introduce you; but that would not be proper for us would it?"

She shook her head positively, "I wouldn't like to do that. He would think I was intruding, I am sure."

"Well then, we will do it this way—the first day that Mr. King and I are both away, and Tee Kee is gone, too; I'll slip out here and leave a letter and a key on your gate. The letter will tell you just the time when we go, and when we will return—so you will know whether it is safe for you or not, and how long you can stay. Only"—he became very serious—"only, you must promise one thing."

"What?"

"That you won't look at the picture on the easel."

"But why must I promise that?"

"Because that picture will not be finished for a long time yet, and you must not look at it until I say it is ready. Mr. King wouldn't like you to see that picture, I am sure. In fact, he doesn't like for any one to see the picture he is working on just now."

"How funny," she said, with a puzzled look. "What is he painting it for? I like for people to hear my music."

The man answered before he thought—"But I don't like people to read my books."

She shrank back, with troubled eyes, "Oh! is he—is he that kind of an artist?"

"No, no, no!" exclaimed the novelist, hastily. "You must not think that. I did not mean you to think that. If he was that kind of an artist, I wouldn't let you go into the studio at all. Mr. King is a good man—the best man I have ever known. He is my friend because he knows the secret about me that you know. He does not read my books. He would not read one of them for anything. It is only that this picture is not finished. When it is finished, he will not care who sees it."

"I'm glad," she said. "You frightened me, for a minute—I understand, now."

"And you promise not to look at the picture on the easel?"

She nodded,—"Of course. And when I come out I'll lock the door and put the key back on the gate again; and no one but you and I will ever know."

"No one but you and I will know," he answered.

As he spoke, Czar, who had been lying quietly in the doorway of the arbor, rose quickly to his feet, with a low growl.

The girl, peering through the screen on the side toward the house, uttered an exclamation of fear and drew back, turning to her companion appealingly. "O please, please don't let that man find me here."

Conrad Lagrauge looked and saw James Rutlidge coming down the path toward the arched entrance to the garden, which was directly across from the arbor.

"Stop him, please stop him," whispered the girl, her hand upon his arm.

"Stay here until I get him out of sight," said the novelist quickly. "I won't let him come into the garden. When we are gone, you can make your escape. Don't forget the music for me, and the key at the gate."

He spoke to Czar, and with the dog obediently at heel went forward to meet Mr. Rutlidge, who had called for Mrs. Taine and Louise.

But all the while that Conrad Lagrange was talking to the man, and leading him toward the door of the studio, he was wondering—why that look of fear upon the face of the girl in the garden? What had Sibyl Andrés to do with James Rutlidge?

Chapter X

A Cry in the Night

As Conrad Lagrange and Mr. Rutlidge entered the studio, Aaron King turned from the easel, where he had drawn the velvet curtain to hide the finished portrait. Mrs. Taine was standing at the other side of the room, wrap in hand, calmly waiting, ready to go. The artist greeted Mr. Rutlidge cordially, while the woman triumphantly announced the completion of her portrait.

"Ah! permit me to congratulate you, old man," said Rutlidge, addressing the artist familiarly. "It is too much, I suppose, to expect a look at it this afternoon?"

"Thanks,"—returned the artist,—"you are all coming to-morrow, at three, you know. I would rather not show it to-day. It is a little late for the best light; and I would like for you to see it under the most favorable conditions possible."

The critic was visibly flattered by the painter's manner and by his well-chosen emphasis upon the personal pronoun. "Quite right"—he said approvingly—"quite right, old boy." He turned to the novelist—"These painter chaps, you know, Lagrange, like to have a few hours for a last touch or two before I come around." He laughed pompously at his own words—the others joining.

When Mrs. Taine and her companions were gone, the artist said hurriedly to his friend, "Come on, let's get it over." He led the way back to the studio.

"I thought the light was too bad," said the older man, quizzingly, as they entered the big room.

"It's good enough for your needs," retorted the painter savagely. "You could see all you want by candle-light." He jerked the curtain angrily aside, and—without a glance at the canvas—walked away to stand at the window looking out upon the rose garden—waiting for the flood of the novelist's scorn to overwhelm him. At last, when no sound broke the quiet of the room, he turned—to find himself alone.

Conrad Lagrange, after one look at the portrait on the easel, had slipped quietly out of the building.

The artist found his friend, a few minutes later, meditatively smoking his pipe on the front porch, with Czar lying at his feet.

"Well," said the painter, curiously,—anxious, as he had said, to have it over,—"why the deuce don't you say something?"

The novelist answered slowly, "My vocabulary is too limited, for one reason, and"—he looked thoughtfully down at Czar—"I prefer to wait until you have finished the portrait."

"It is finished," returned the artist desperately. "I swear I'll never touch a brush to the damned thing again."

The man with the pipe spoke to the dog at his feet; "Listen to him, Czar—listen to the poor devil of a painter-man."

The dog arose, and, placing his head upon his master's knee, looked up into the lined and rugged face, as the novelist continued, "If he was only a wee bit puffed up and cocky over the thing, now, we could exert ourselves, so we could, couldn't we?" Czar slowly waved a feathery tail in dignified approval. His master continued, "But when a fellow can do a crime like that, and still retain enough virtue in his heart to hear his work shrieking to heaven its curses upon him for calling it into existence, it's best for outsiders to keep quite still. Your poor old master knows whereof he speaks, doesn't he, dog? That he does!"

"And is that all you have to say on the subject?" demanded the artist, as though for some reason he was disappointed at his friend's reticence.

"I might add a word of advice," said the other.

"Well, what is it?"

"That you pray your gods—if you have any—to be merciful, and bestow upon you either less genius or more intelligence to appreciate it."

At three o'clock, the following afternoon, the little party from Fairlands Heights came to view, the portrait Or,—as Conrad Lagrange said, while the automobile was approaching the house, "Well, here they come—'The Age', accompanied by 'Materialism', 'Sensual', and 'Ragtime'—to look upon the prostitution of Art, and call it good." Escorted by the artist, and the novelist, they went at once to the studio.

The appreciation of the picture was instantaneous—so instantaneous, in fact, that Louise Taine's lips were shaped to deliver an expressive "oh" of admiration, even before the portrait was revealed. As though the painter, in drawing back the easel curtain, gave an appointed signal, that "oh" was set off with the suddenness of a sky-rocket's rush, and was accompanied in its flight by a great volume of sizzling, sputtering, glittering, adjectival sparks that—filling the air to no purpose whatever—winked out as they were born; the climax of the pyrotechnical display being reached in the explosive pop of another "oh" which released a brilliant shower of variegated sighs and moans and ecstatic looks and inarticulate exclamations—ending, of course, in total darkness.

Mrs. Taine hastened to turn the artist's embarrassed attention to an appreciation that had the appearance, at least, of a more enduring value. Drawing, with affectionate solicitude, close to her husband, she asked,—in a voice that was tremulous with loving care and anxiety to please,—"Do you like it, dear?"

"It is magnificent, splendid, perfect!" This effort to give his praise of the artist's work the appearance of substantial reality cost the wretched product of lust and luxury a fit of coughing that racked his burnt-out body almost to its last feeble hold upon the world of flesh and, with a force that shamed the strength of his words, drove home the truth that neither his praise nor his scorn could long endure. When he could again speak, he said, in his husky, rasping whisper,—while grasping the painter's hand in effusive cordiality,—"My dear fellow, I congratulate you. It is exquisite. It will create a sensation, sir, when it is exhibited. Your fame is assured. I must thank you for the honor you have done me in thus immortalizing the beauty and character of Mrs. Taine." And then, to his wife,—"Dearest, I am glad for you, and proud. It is as worthy of you as paint and canvas could be." He turned to Conrad Lagrange who was an interested observer of the scene—"Am I not right, Lagrange?"

"Quite right, Mr. Taine,—quite right. As you say, the portrait is most worthy the beauty and character of the charming subject."

Another paroxysm of coughing mercifully prevented the poor creature's reply.

With one accord, the little group turned, now, to James Rutlidge—the dreaded authority and arbiter of artistic destinies. That distinguished expert, while the others were speaking, had been listening intently; ostensibly, the while, he examined the picture with a show of trained skill that, it seemed, could not fail to detect unerringly those more subtle values and defects that are popularly supposed to be hidden from the common eye. Silently, in breathless awe, they watched the process by which professional criticism finds its verdict. That is, they thought they were watching the process. In reality, the method is more subtle than they knew.

While the great critic moved back and forth in front of the easel; drew away from or bent over to closely scrutinize the canvas; shifted the easel a hair breadth several times; sat down; stood erect; hummed and muttered to himself abstractedly; cleared his throat with an impressive "Ahem"; squinted through nearly closed eyes, with his head thrown back, or turned in every side angle his fat neck would permit: peered through his half-closed fist; peeped through funnels of paper; sighted over and under his open hand or a paper held to shut out portions of the painting;—the others thought they saw him expertly weighing the evidence for and against the merit of the work. In reality it was his ears and not his eyes that helped the critic to his final decision—a decision which was delivered, at last, with a convincing air of ponderous finality. Indeed it was a judgment from which there could be no appeal, for it expressed exactly the views of those for whose benefit it was rendered. Then, in a manner subtly insinuating himself into the fellowship of the famous, he, too, turned to Conrad Lagrange with a scholarly; "Do you not agree, sir?"

The novelist answered with slow impressiveness; "The picture, undoubtedly, fully merits the appreciation and praise you have given it. I have already congratulated Mr. King—who was kind enough to show me his work before you arrived."

After this, Yee Kee appeared upon the scene, and tea was served in the studio—a fitting ceremony to the launching of another genius.

"By the way, Mr. Lagrange," said Mrs. Taine, quite casually,—when, under the influence of the mildly stimulating beverage, the talk had assumed a more frivolous vein,—"Who is your talented neighbor that so charms Mr. King with the music of a violin?"

The novelist, as he turned toward the speaker, shot a quick glance at the Artist. Nor did those keen, baffling eyes fail to note that, at the question, James Rutlidge had paused in the middle of a sentence. "That is one of the mysteries of our romantic surroundings madam," said Conrad Lagrange, easily.

"And a very charming mystery it seems to be," returned the woman. "It has been quite affecting to watch its influence upon Mr. King."

The artist laughed. "I admit that I found the music, in combination with the beauty I have so feebly tried to out upon canvas, very stimulating."

A flash of angry color swept into the perfect cheeks of Mrs. Taine, as she retorted with meaning; "You are as flattering in your speech as you are with your brush. I assure you I do not consider myself in your unknown musician's class."

The small eyes of James Rutlidge were fixed inquiringly upon the speakers, while his heavy face betrayed—to the watchful novelist—an interest he could not hide. "Is this music of such exceptional merit?" he asked with an attempt at indifference.

Louise Taine—sensing that the performances of the unnamed violinist had been acceptable to Conrad Lagrange and Aaron King—the two representatives of the world to which she aspired—could not let the opportunity slip. She fairly deluged them with the spray of her admiring ejaculations in praise of the musician—employing, hit or miss, every musical term that popped into her vacuous head.

"Indeed,"—said the critic,—"I seem to have missed a treat." Then, directly to the artist,—"And you say the violinist is wholly unknown to you?"

"Wholly," returned the painter, shortly.

Conrad Lagrange saw a faint smile of understanding and disbelief flit for an instant over the heavy face of James Rutlidge.

When the automobile, at last, was departing with the artist's guests; the two friends stood for a moment watching it up the road to the west, toward town. As the big car moved away, they saw Mrs. Taine lean forward to speak to the chauffeur while James Rutlidge, who was in the front seat, turned and shook his head as though in protest. The woman appeared to insist. The machine slowed down, as though the chauffeur, in doubt, awaited the outcome of the discussion. Then, just in front of that neighboring house, Rutlidge seemed to yield abruptly, and the automobile turned suddenly in toward the curb and stopped. Mrs. Taine alighted, and disappeared in the depths of the orange grove.

Aaron King and Conrad Lagrange looked at each other, for a moment, in questioning silence. The artist laughed. "Our poor little mystery," he said.

But the novelist—as they went toward the house—cursed Mrs. Taine, James Rutlidge, and all their kin and kind, with a vehement earnestness that startled his companion—familiar as the latter was with his friend's peculiar talent in the art of vigorous expression.

After dinner, that evening, the painter and the novelist sat on the porch—as their custom was—to watch the day go out of the sky and the night come over valley and hill and mountain until, above the highest peaks, the stars of God looked down upon the twinkling lights of the towns of men. At that hour, too, it was the custom, now, for the violinist hidden in the orange grove, to make the music they both so loved.

In the music, that night, there was a feeling that, to them, was new—a vague, uncertain, halting undertone that was born, they felt, of fear. It stirred them to question and to wonder. Without apparent cause or reason, they each oddly connected the troubled tone in the music with the stopping of the automobile from Fairlands Heights, that afternoon, at the gate of the little house next door—the artist, because of Mrs. Taine's insistent inquiry about the, to him, unknown musician;—Conrad Lagrange, because of the manner of the girl in the garden when James Rutlidge appeared and because of the critic's interest when they had spoken of the violinist in the studio. But neither expressed his thought to the other.

Presently, the music ceased, and they sat for an hour, perhaps, in silence—as close friends may do—exchanging only now and then a word.

Suddenly, they were startled by a cry. In the still darkness of the night, from the mysterious depths of the orange grove, the sound came with such a shock that the two men, for the moment, held their places, motionless—questioning each other sharply—"What was that?" "Did you hear?"—as though they doubted, almost, their own ears.

The cry came again; this time, undoubtedly, from that neighboring house to the west. It was unmistakably the cry of a woman—a woman in fear and pain.

They leaped to their feet.

Again the cry came from the black depths of the orange grove—shuddering, horrible—in an agony of fear.

The two men sprang from the porch, and, through the darkness that in the orange grove was like a black wall, ran toward the spot from which the sound came—the dog at their heels.

Breathless, they broke into the little yard in front of the tiny box-like house. Lights shone in the windows. All seemed peaceful and still. Czar betrayed no uneasiness. Going to the front door, they knocked.

There was no answer save the sound of some one moving inside.

Again, the artist knocked vigorously.

The door opened, and a woman stood on the threshold.

Standing a little to one side, the men saw her features clearly, in the light from the room. It was the woman with the disfigured face.

Conrad Lagrange was first to command himself. "I beg your pardon, madam. We live in the house next door. We thought we heard a cry of distress. May we offer our assistance in any way? Is there anything we can do?"

"Thank you, sir, you are very kind,"—returned the woman, in a low voice,—"but it is nothing. There is nothing you can do."

And the voice of Sibyl Andrés, who stood farther back in the room, where the artist from his position could not see her, added, "It was good of you to come, Mr. Lagrange; but it is really nothing. We are so sorry you were disturbed."

"Not at all," returned the men, as the woman of the disfigured face drew back from the door. "Good night."

"Good night," came from within the house, and the door was shut.

Chapter XI

Go Look In Your Mirror, You Fool

As the Taine automobile left Aaron King and his friend, that afternoon, Mrs. Taine spoke to the chauffeur; "You may stop a moment, at the next house, Henry."

If she had fired a gun, James Rutlidge could not have turned with a more startled suddenness.

"What in thunder do you want there?" he demanded shortly.

"I want to stop," she returned calmly.

"But I must get down town, at once," he protested. "I have already lost the best part of the afternoon."

"Your business seems to have become important very suddenly," she observed, sarcastically.

"I have something to do besides making calls with you," he retorted. "Go on, Henry."

Mrs. Taine spoke sharply; "Really, Jim, you are going too far. Henry, turn in at the house." The machine moved toward the curb and stopped. As she stepped from the car, she added, "I will only be a minute, Jim."

Rutlidge growled an inarticulate curse.

"What deviltry do you suppose she is up to now," rasped Mr. Taine.

Which brought from his daughter the usual protest,—"O, papa, don't,"

As Mrs. Taine approached the house, Sibyl Andrés—busy among the flowers that bordered the walk—heard the woman's step, and stood quietly waiting her. Mrs. Taine's face was perfect in its expression of cordial interest, with just enough—but not too much—of a conscious, well-bred superiority. The girl's countenance was lighted by an expression of childlike surprise and wonder. What had brought this well-known leader in the social world from Fairlands Heights to the poor, little house in the orange grove, so far down the hill?

"Good afternoon," said the caller. "You are Miss Andrés, are you not?"

"Yes," returned the girl, with a smile. "Won't you come in? I will call Miss Willard."

"Oh, thank you, no. I have only a moment. My friends are waiting. I am Mrs. Taine."

"Yes, I know. I have often seen you passing."

The other turned abruptly. "What beautiful flowers."

"Aren't they lovely," agreed Sibyl, with frank pleasure at the visitor's appreciation. "Let me give you a bunch." Swiftly she gathered a generous armful.

Mrs. Taine protested, but the girl presented her offering with such grace and winsomeness that the other could not refuse. As she received the gift, the perfect features of the woman of the world were colored by a blush that even she could not control. "I understand, Miss Andrés," she said, "that you are an accomplished violinist."

"I teach and play in Park Church," was the simple answer.

"I have never happened to hear you, myself,"—said Mrs. Taine smoothly,—"but my friends who live next door—Mr. Lagrange and Mr. King—have told me about you."

"Oh!" The girl's voice was vaguely troubled, while the other, watching, saw the blush that colored her warmly tinted cheeks.

"It is good of you to play for them," continued the woman from Fairlands Heights, casually. "You must enjoy the society of such famous men, very much. There are a great many people, you know, who would envy you your friendship with them."

The girl replied quickly, "O, but you are mistaken. I am not acquainted with them, at all; that is—not with Mr. King—I have never spoken to him—and I only met Mr. Lagrange, for a few minutes, by accident."

"Indeed! But I am forgetting the purpose of my call, and my friends will become impatient. Do you ever play for private entertainments, Miss Andrés?—for—say a dinner, or a reception, you know?"

"I would be very glad for such an engagement, Mrs. Taine. I must earn what I can with my music, and there are not enough pupils to occupy all my time. But perhaps you should hear me play, first. I will get my violin."

Mrs. Taine checked her, "Oh, no, indeed. It is quite unnecessary, my dear. The opinion of your distinguished neighbors is quite enough. I shall keep you in mind for some future occasion. I just wished to learn if you would accept such an engagement. Good-by. Thanks—so much—for your flowers."

She was upon the point of turning away, when a low cry from the nearby porch startled them both. Turning, they saw the woman with the disfigured face, standing in the doorway; an expression of mingled wonder, love, and supplication upon her hideously marred features. As they looked, she started toward them,—impulsively stretching out her arms, as though the gesture was an involuntary expression of some deep emotion,—then checked herself, suddenly as though in doubt.

Sibyl Andrés uttered an exclamation. "Why, Myra! what is it, dear?"

Mrs. Taine turned away with a gesture of horror, saying to the girl in a low, hurried voice, "Dear me, how dreadful! I really must be going."

As she went down the flower-bordered path towards the street, the woman on the porch, again, stretched out her arms appealingly. Then, as Sibyl reached her side, the poor creature clasped the girl in a close embrace, and burst into bitter tears.

Upon the return of the Taines and James Rutlidge to the house on Fairlands Heights, Mrs. Taine retired immediately to her own luxuriously appointed apartments.

At dinner, a maid brought to the household word that her mistress was suffering from a severe headache and would not be down and begged that she might not be disturbed during the evening.

Alone in her room, Mrs. Taine—her headache being wholly conventional—gave herself unreservedly to the thoughts that she could not, under the eyes of others, entertain without restraint. She was seated at a window that looked down upon the carefully graded levels of the envying Fairlanders and across the wide sweep of the valley below to the mountains which, from that lofty point of vantage, could be seen from the base of their lowest foothills to the crests of their highest peaks. But the woman who lived on the Heights of Fairlands saw neither the homes of their neighbors, the busy valley below, nor the mountains that lifted so far above them all. Her thoughts were centered upon what, to her, was more than these.

When night was gathering over the scene, her maid entered softly. Mrs. Taine dismissed the woman with a word, telling her not to return until she rang. Leaving the window, after drawing the shades close, she paced the now lighted room, in troubled uneasiness of mind. Here and there, she paused to touch or handle some familiar object—a photograph in a silver frame, a book on the carved table, the trifles on her open desk, or an ornamental vase on the mantle—then moved restlessly away to continue her aimless exercise. When the silence was rudely broken by the sound of a knock at her door, she stood still—a look of anger marring the well-schooled beauty of her features.

The knock was repeated.

With an exclamation of impatient annoyance, she crossed the room, and flung open the door.

Without leave or apology, her husband entered; and, as he did so, was seized by a paroxysm of coughing that sent him reeling, gasping and breathless, to the nearest chair.

Mrs. Taine stood watching her husband coldly, with a curious, speculative expression on her face that she made no attempt to hide. When his torture was abated—for the time—leaving him exhausted and trembling with weakness, she said coldly, "Well, what do you want? What are you doing here?"

The man lifted his pallid, haggard face and, with a yellow, claw-like hand wiped the beads of clammy sweat from his forehead; while his deep-sunken eyes leered at her with an insane light.

The woman was at no pains to conceal her disgust. In her voice there was no hint of pity. "Didn't Marie tell you that I wished to be alone?"

"Of course," he jeered in his rasping whisper, "that's why I came." He gave a hideous resemblance to a laugh, which ended in a cough—and, again, he drew his skinny, shaking hand across his damp forehead "That's the time that a man should visit his wife, isn't it? When she is alone. Or"—he grinned mockingly—"when she wishes to be?"

She regarded him with open scorn and loathing. "You unclean beast! Will you take yourself out of my room?"

He gazed at her, as a malevolent devil might gloat over a soul delivered up for torture. "Not until I choose to go, my dear."

[Illustration: "Well, what do you want? What are you doing here?"]

Suddenly changing her manner, she smiled with deliberate, mocking humor. While he watched, she moved leisurely to a deep, many-cushioned couch; and, arranging the pillows, reclined among them in the careless abandonment of voluptuous ease and physical content. Openly, ostentatiously, she exhibited herself to his burning gaze in various graceful poses—lifting her arms above her head to adjust a cushion more to her liking; turning and stretching her beautiful body; moving her limbs with sinuous enjoyment—as disregardful of his presence as though she were alone. At last she spoke in cool, even, colorless tones; "Perhaps you will tell me what you want?"

The wretched victim of his own unbridled sensuality shook with inarticulate rage. Choking and coughing he writhed in his chair—his emaciated limbs twisted grotesquely; his sallow face bathed in perspiration his claw-like hands opening and closing; his bloodless lips curled back from his yellow teeth, in a horrid grin of impotent fury. And all the while she lay watching him with that pitiless, mocking, smile. It was as though the malevolent devil and the tortured soul had suddenly changed places.

When the man could speak, he reviled her, in his rasping whisper, with curses that it seemed must blister his tongue. She received his effort with jeering laughter and taunting words; moving her body, now and then, among the cushions, with an air of purely physical enjoyment that, to the other, was maddening.

"If this is all you came for,"—she said, easily,—"might have spared yourself the effort—don't you think?"

Controlling himself, in a measure, he returned, "I came to tell you that your intimacy with that damned painter must stop."

Her eyes narrowed slightly. One hand, hidden in the cushions, clenched until her rings hurt. "Just what do you mean by my intimacy?" she asked evenly.

"You know what I mean," he replied coarsely. "I mean what intimacy with a man always means to a woman like you."

"The only meaning that a creature of your foul mind can understand," she retorted smoothly. "If it were worth while to tell you the truth, I would say that my conduct when alone with Mr. King has been as proper as—as when I am alone with you."

The taunt maddened him. Interrupted by spells of coughing—choking, gasping, fighting for breath, his eyes blazing with hatred and lust, mingling his words with oaths and curses—he raged at her. "And do you think—that, because I am so nearly dead,—I do not resent what—I saw, to-day? Do you think—I am so far gone that I cannot—understand—your interest in this man,—after—watching you, together, all—the afternoon? Has there been any one—in his studio, except you two, when—he was painting you in that dress—which you—designed for his benefit? Oh, no, indeed,—you and your—genius could not be interrupted,—for the sake—of his art. His art! Great God!—was there ever such a damnable farce—since hell was invented? Art!—you—you—you!—" crazed with jealous fury, he pointed at her with his yellow, shaking, skeleton fingers; and struggled to raise his voice above that rasping whisper until the cords of his scrawny neck stood out and his face was distorted with the strain of his effort—"You! painted as a—modest Quaker Maid,—with all the charm of innocence,—virtue, and religious piety in your face. You! And that picture will be exhibited—and written about—as a work of art! You'll pull all the strings,—and use all your influence,—and the thing—will be received as a—masterpiece."

"And," she added calmly, "you will write a check—and lie, as you did this afternoon."

Without heeding her remark, he went on,—"You know the picture is worthless. He knows it,—Conrad Lagrange knows it,—Jim Rutlidge knows it,—the whole damned clique and gang of you know it, He's like all his kind,—a pretender,—a poser,—playing into the hands—of such women as you; to win social position—and wealth. And we and our kind—we pretend to believe—in such damned parasites,—and exalt them and what we—call their art,—and keep them in luxury, and buy their pictures;—because they prostitute—their talents to gratify our vanity. We know it's all a damned sham—and a pretense that if they were real artists,—with an honest workman's respect for their work,—they wouldn't—recognize us."

"Don't forget to send him a check,"—she murmured—"you can't afford to neglect it, you know—think how people would talk."

"Don't worry," he replied. "There'll be no talk. I'll send the genius his check—for making love—to my wife in the sacred name of art,—and I'll lie—about his picture with—the rest of you. But there will be—no more of your intimacy with him. You're my wife,—in spite of hell,—and from now on—I'll see—that you are true—to me. Your sickening pose—of modesty in dress shall be something—more than a pose. For the little time I have left,—I'll have—you to—myself or I'll kill you."

His reference to her refusal to uncover her shoulders in public broke the woman's calm and aroused her to a cold fury. Springing to her feet, she stood over him as he sat huddled in his chair, exhausted by his effort.

"What is your silly, idle threat beside the fact," she said with stinging scorn. "To have killed me, instead of making me your wife, would have been a kindness greater than you are capable of. You know how unspeakably vile you were when you bought me. You know how every hour of my life with you has been a torment to me. You should be grateful that I have helped you to live your lie—that I have played the game of respectability with you—that I am willing to play it a little while longer, until you lay down your hand for good, and release us both.

"Suppose I were what you think me? What right have you to object to my pleasures? Have you—in all your life of idle, vicious, luxury—have you ever feared to do evil if it appealed to your bestial nature? You know you have not. You have feared only the appearance of evil. To be as evil as you like so long as you can avoid the appearance of evil; that's the game you have taught me to play. That's the game we have played together. That's the game we and our kind insist the artists and writers shall help us play. That's the only game I know, and, by the rule of our game, so long as the world sees nothing, I shall do what pleases me.

"You have had your day with me. You have had what you paid for. What right have you to deny me, now, an hour's forgetfulness? When I think of what I might have been, but for you, I wonder that I have cared to live, and I would not—except for the poor sport of torturing you.

"You scoff at Mr. King's portrait of me because he has not painted me as I am! What would you have said if he had painted me as I am? What would you say if Conrad Lagrange should write the truth about us and our kind, for his millions of readers? You sneer at me because I cannot uncover my shoulders in the conventional dress of my class, and so make a virtue of a necessity and deceive the world by a pretense of modesty. Go look in your mirror, you fool! Your right to sneer at me for my poor little pretense is denied you by every line of your repulsive countenance Now get out. I'm going to retire."

And she rang for her maid.

Chapter XII

First Fruits of His Shame

When the postman, in his little cart, stopped at the home of Aaron King and his friend, that day, it was Conrad Lagrange who received the mail. The artist was in his studio, and the novelist, knowing that the painter was not at work, went to him there with a letter.

The portrait—still on the easel—was hidden by the velvet curtain. Sitting by a table that was littered with a confusion of sketches, books and papers, the young man was re-tying a package of old letters that he had, evidently, just been reading.

As the novelist went to him, the artist said quietly,—indicating the package in his hand,—"From my mother. She wrote them during the last year of my study abroad." When the other did not reply, he continued thoughtfully, "Do you know, Lagrange, since my acquaintance with you, I find many things in these old letters that—at the time I received them—I did not, at all, appreciate. You seem to be helping me, somehow, to a better understanding of my mother's spirit and mind." He smiled.

Presently, Conrad Lagrange, when he could trust himself to speak, said, "Your mother's mind and spirit, Aaron, were too fine and rare to be fully appreciated or understood except by one trained in the school of life, itself. When she wrote those letters, you were a student of mere craftsmanship. She, herself no doubt, recognized that you would not fully comprehend the things she wrote; but she put them down, out of the very fullness of her intellectual and spiritual wealth—trusting to your love to preserve the letters, and to the years to give you understanding."

"Why," cried the artist, "those are almost her exact words—as I have just been reading them!"

The other, smiling, continued quietly, "Your appreciation and understanding of your mother will continue to grow through all your life, Aaron. When you are old—as old as I am—you will still find in those letters hidden treasures of thought, and truths of greater value than you, now, can realize. But here—I have brought you your share of the afternoon's mail."

When Aaron King opened the envelope that his friend laid on the table before him, he sat regarding its contents with an air of thoughtful meditation—lost to his surroundings.

The novelist—who had gone to the window and was looking into the rose garden—turned to speak to his friend; but the other did not reply. Again, the man at the window addressed the painter; but still the younger man was silent. At this, Conrad Lagrange came back to the table; an expression of anxiety upon his face. "What is it, old man? What's the matter? No bad news, I hope?"

Aaron King, aroused from his fit of abstraction, laughed shortly, and held out to his friend the letter he had just received. It was from Mr. Taine. Enclosed was the millionaire's check. The letter was a formal business note; the check was for an amount that drew a low whistle from the novelist's lips.

"Rather higher pay than old brother Judas received for a somewhat similar service, isn't it," he commented, as he passed the letter and check back to the artist. Then, as he watched the younger man's face, he asked, "What's the matter, don't you like the flavor of these first fruits of your shame? I advise you to cultivate a taste for this sort of thing as quickly as possible—in your own defense."

"Don't you think you are a little bit too hard on us all, Lagrange?" asked the artist, with a faint smile. "These people are satisfied. The picture pleases them."

"Of course they are pleased," retorted the other. "You know your business. That's the trouble with you. That's the trouble with us all, these days—we painters and writers and musicians—we know our business too damned well. We have the mechanics of our crafts, the tricks of our trades, so well in hand that we make our books and pictures and music say what we please. We use our art to gain our own vain ends instead of being driven by our art to find adequate expression for some great truth that demands through us a hearing. You have said it all, my friend—you have summed up the whole situation in the present-day world of creative art—these people are satisfied. You have given them what they want, prostituting your art to do it. That's what I have been doing all these years—giving people what they want. For a price we cater to them—even as their tailors, and milliners, and barbers. And never again will the world have a truly great art or literature until men like us—in the divine selfishness of their, calling—demand, first and last, that they, themselves, be satisfied by the work of their hands."

Going to the easel, he rudely jerked aside the curtain. Involuntarily, the painter went to stand by his side before the picture.

"Look at it!" cried the novelist. "Look at it in the light of your own genius! Don't you see its power? Doesn't it tell you what you could do, if you would? If you couldn't paint a picture, or if you couldn't feel a picture to be painted, it wouldn't matter. I'd let you ride to hell on your own palette, and be damned to you. But this thing shows a power that the world can ill afford to lose. It is so bad because it is so good. Come here!" he drew his friend to the big window, and pointed to the mountains. "There is an art like those mountains, my boy—lonely, apart from the world; remotely above the squalid ambitions of men; Godlike in its calm strength and peace—an art to which men may look for inspiration and courage and hope. And there is an art that is like Fairlands—petty and shallow and mean—with only the fictitious value that its devotees assume, but never, actually, realize. Listen, Aaron, don't continue to misread your mother's letters. Don't misunderstand her as thinking that the place she coveted for you is a place within the power of these people to give. Come with me into the mountains, yonder. Come, and let us see if, in those hills of God, you cannot find yourself."

When Conrad Lagrange finished, the artist stood, for a little, without reply—irresolute, before his picture—the check in his hand. At last, still without speaking, he went back to the table, where he wrote briefly his reply to Mr. Taine. When he had finished, he handed his letter to the older man, who read:

Dear Sir:

In reply to yours of the 13th, inst., enclosing your check in payment   for the portrait of Mrs. Taine; I appreciate your generosity, but   cannot, now, accept it.

I find, upon further consideration, that the portrait does not fully   satisfy me. I shall, therefore, keep the canvas until I can, with the   consent of my own mind, put my signature upon it.

Herewith, I am returning your check; for, of course, I cannot accept   payment for an unfinished work.

In a day or two, Mr. Lagrange and I will start to the mountains, for an   outing. Trusting that you and your family will enjoy the season at Lake   Silence I am, with kind regards,

Yours sincerely, Aaron King.

That evening, the two men talked over their proposed trip, and laid their plans to start without delay As Conrad Lagrange put it—they would lose themselves in the hills; with no definite destination in view; and no set date for their return. Also, he stipulated that they should travel light—with only a pack burro to carry their supplies—and that they should avoid the haunts of the summer resorters, and keep to the more unfrequented trails. The novelist's acquaintance with the country into which they would go, and his experience in woodcraft—gained upon many like expeditions in the lonely wilds he loved—would make a guide unnecessary. It would be a new experience for Aaron King; and, as the novelist talked, he found himself eager as a schoolboy for the trip; while the distant mountains, themselves, seemed to call him—inviting him to learn the secret of their calm strength and the spirit of their lofty peace. The following day, they would spend in town; purchasing an outfit of the necessary equipment and supplies, securing a burro, and attending to numerous odds and ends of business preparatory to their indefinite absence.

It so happened, the next day, that Yee Kee,—who was to care for the place during their weeks of absence had matters of importance to himself, that demanded his attention in town. When his masters informed him that they would not be home for lunch, he took advantage of the opportunity and asked for the day.

Thus it came about that Conrad Lagrange—in the spirit of a boy bent upon some secret adventure— stole out into the rose garden, that morning, to leave the promised letter and key at the little gate in the corner of the Ragged Robin hedge.

Chapter XIII

Myra Willard's Challenge

Since her meeting with Conrad Lagrange in the rose garden, Sibyl Andrés had looked, every day, for that promised letter. She found it early in the afternoon. It was a quaint letter—written in the spirit of their meeting—telling her the probable time of her neighbor's return; warning her, in fear of some fanciful horror, to beware of the picture on the easel; and wishing her joy of the adventure. With the note, was a key.

A few minutes later, the girl unlocked the door of the studio, and entered the building that had once been so familiar to her, but was now, in its interior, so transformed. Slowly, she pushed the door to, behind her. As though half frightened at her own daring, she stood quite still, looking about. In the atmosphere of that somewhat richly furnished apartment; poised timidly as if for ready flight; she seemed, indeed, the spirit that the novelist—in playful fancy—insisted that she was. Her cheeks were glowing with color; her eyes were bright with the excitement of her innocent adventure, and with her genuine admiration and appreciation of the beautiful room.

Presently,—growing bolder,—she began moving about the studio—light-footed and graceful as a wild thing from her own mountain home, and, indeed, with much the air of a gentle creature of the woods that had strayed into the haunts of men. Intensely interested in the things she found, she gradually forgot her timidity, and gave herself to the enjoyment of her surroundings, with the freedom and abandon of a child. From picture to picture, she went, with wide, eager eyes. She turned over the sketches in the big portfolios that were so invitingly open; looked with awe upon the brushes stuck in the big Chinese jar—upon the palettes, and at the tubes of color; flitting to the window that looked out upon her garden, and back to the great, north light with its view of the distant mountains; and again and again, paused to stand with her hands clasped behind her, in front of the big easel with its canvas hidden under the velvet curtain. Then she must try the chairs, the oriental couch, and even the stool— where she had seen the artist sitting, sometimes, at his work, when she had watched him from the arbor; and last—in a pretty make believe—she tried the seat on the model throne, as though posing herself, for her portrait.

Suddenly, with a startled cry, she sprang to her feet; then shrank back, white and trembling—her big eyes fixed with pleading fear upon the man who stood in the open doorway, regarding her with a curious, triumphant smile. It was James Rutlidge.

Sibyl, occupied with her childlike delight, had failed to hear the automobile when it stopped in front of the house. Finding no one in the house the man had gone on to the studio, where—with the assurance of an intimate acquaintance—he had pushed open the door that was standing ajar.

At the girl's frightened manner, the man laughed. Closing the door, he said, with an insinuating sneer, "You were not expecting me, it seems."

His words aroused Sibyl from her momentary weakness. Rising, she said calmly, "I was not expecting any one, Mr. Rutlidge."

Again he laughed—with unpleasant meaning. "You certainly look to be very much at home." He moved confidently to the easel stool and, seating himself continued with a leering smile, "What's the matter with my taking the artist's place for a little while—at least, until he comes?"

The girl was too innocent to understand his assumption but her pure mind could not fail to sense the evil in his words.

"I had permission to come here this afternoon," she said—her voice trembling a little with the fear that she did not understand. "Won't you go, please? Neither Mr. King nor Mr. Lagrange are at home."

"I do not doubt your having permission to come here," he returned, with meaning stress upon the word, "permission". "I see you even carry a key to this really delightful room." He motioned with his head toward the door where he had seen the key in the lock, as she had left it.

At this, she grasped a hint of the man's thought and, for an instant, drew hack in shame. Then, suddenly with a burst of indignant anger, she took a step toward him, demanding clearly; "Are you saying that I am in the habit of coming here to meet Mr. King?"

He laughed mockingly. "Really, my dear, no one, seeing you, now, could blame the man for giving you a key to this place where he is popularly supposed to be undisturbed. Mr. King is neither such a virtuous saint, nor so engrossed in his art, as to resent the companionship of such a vision of loveliness—simply because it comes in the form of good flesh and blood. Why be angry with me?"

Her cheeks were crimson as she said, again, "Will you go?"

"Not until you have settled the terms of peace," he answered with that leering smile. "Fortune has favored me, this afternoon, and I mean to profit by it."

For an instant, she looked at him—frightened and dismayed. Suddenly, with the flash-like quickness that was a part of her physical inheritance from her mountain life, she darted past him; eluding his effort to detain her—and was out of the building.

With an oath, the man, acting upon the impulse of the moment, ran after her. Outside the door of the studio, he caught a glimpse of her white dress as she disappeared into the rose garden. In the garden, he saw her as she slipped through the little gate in the far corner of the hedge, into the orange grove. Recklessly he followed. Among the trees, he glimpsed, again, the white flash of her skirts, and dashed forward. At the farther edge of the grove that walled in the little yard where Sibyl lived, he saw her standing by the kitchen door. But between the girl and that last row of close-set trees, waiting his coming, stood the woman with the disfigured face.

Rutlidge paused—angry with himself for so foolishly yielding to the impulse of his passion.

Myra Willard went toward him fearlessly—her fine eyes blazing with righteous indignation. "What are you trying to do, James Rutlidge?" she demanded—and her words were bold and clear.

The man was silent.

"You are evidently a worthy son of your father," the woman continued—every clear-cut word biting into his consciousness with stinging scorn. "He, in his day, did all he knew to turn this world into a hell for those who were unfortunate enough to please his vile fancy. You, I see, are following faithfully his footsteps. I know you, and the creed of your kind—as I knew your father before you. No girl of innocent beauty is safe from you. Your unclean mind is as incapable of believing in virtue, as you are helpless in the grip of your own insane lust."

The man was stung to fury by her cutting words. "Take your ugly face out of my sight," he said brutally.

Fearlessly, she drew a step nearer. "It is because I am a woman that I have this ugly face, James Rutlidge." She touched her disfigured cheek—"These scars are the marks of the beast that rules you, sir, body and soul. Leave this place, or, as there is a God, I'll tell a tale that will forbid you ever showing your own evil countenance in public, again."

Something in her eyes and in her manner, as she spoke, caused the man—beside himself with rage, as he was—to draw back. Some mysterious force that made itself felt in her bold words told him that hers was no idle threat. A moment they stood face to face, in the edge of the shadowy orange grove—the man of the world, prominent in circles of art and culture; and the woman whose natural loveliness was so distorted into a hideous mask of ugliness. With a short, derisive laugh, James Rutlidge turned and walked away.

Aaron King and Conrad Lagrange were returning from town. As they neared their home, they saw one of the Taine automobiles in front of the house. "Company," said the artist with a smile—thinking of his letter to the millionaire.

"It's Rutlidge," said the novelist—noting the absence of the chauffeur.

They were turning in at the entrance, when Czar—who had dashed ahead as if to investigate—halted, suddenly, with a low growl of disapproval.

"Huh!" ejaculated Conrad Lagrange, with his twisted grin. "It's Senior 'Sensual' all right. Look at Czar; he knows the beast is around. Go fetch him, Czar."

With an angry bark, the dog disappeared around the corner of the porch. The two men, following, were met by Rutlidge who had made his way back through the grove and the rose garden from the house next door. The dog, with muttering growls, was sniffing suspiciously at his heels.

"Czar," said his master, suggestively. With a meaning glance, the dog reluctantly ceased his embarrassing attentions and went to see if everything was all right about the premises.

In answer to their greeting and the quite natural question if he had been waiting long, Rutlidge answered with a laugh. "Oh, no—I have been amusing myself by prowling around your place. Snug quarters you have here; really, I never quite appreciated their charm, before."

They seated themselves on the porch. Conrad Lagrange—thinking of Sibyl Andrés and that letter which he had left on the gate—from under his brows, watched their caller closely; the while he filled with painstaking care his brier pipe.

"We like it," returned the artist.

"I should think so—I'd be sorry to leave it if I were you. Mr. Taine tells me you are going to the mountains."

"We're not giving up this place, though," replied Aaron King. "Yee Kee stays to take care of things until our return."

"Oh, I see. I generally go into the mountains, myself for a little hunt when the deer season opens. It may be that I will run across you somewhere. By the way—you haven't met your musical neighbor yet, have you?"

The novelist gave particular attention to his pipe which did not seem to be behaving properly.

The artist answered shortly, "No."

"I'd certainly make her acquaintance, if I were you," said Rutlidge, with his suggestive smile. "She is a dream. A delightful little retreat—that studio of yours."

The painter, puzzled by the man's words and by his insinuating air, returned coldly, "It does very well for a work-shop."

The other laughed meaningly; "Yes, oh yes—a great little work-shop. I suppose you—ah—do not fear to trust your art treasures to the Chinaman, during your absence?"

Conrad Lagrange—certain, now, that the man had seen Sibyl Andrés either entering or leaving the studio—said abruptly, "You need give yourself no concern for Mr. King's studio, Rutlidge. I can assure you that the treasures there will be well protected."

James Rutlidge understood the warning conveyed in the novelist's words that, to Aaron King, revealed nothing.

"Really," said the painter to their caller, "you are not uneasy for the safety of Mrs. Taine's portrait, are you, old man? If you are, of course—"

"Damn Mrs. Taine's portrait!" ejaculated the man, rising hurriedly. "You know what I mean. It's all right, of course. I must be going. Hope you have a good outing and come back to find all your art treasures safe." He laughed coarsely, as he went down the walk.

When the automobile was gone, the artist turned to his friend. "Now what in thunder did he mean by that? What's the matter with him? Do you suppose they imagine that there is anything wrong because I wouldn't turn over the picture?"

"He is an unclean beast, Aaron," the novelist answered shortly. "His father was the worst I ever knew, and he's like him. Forget him. Here comes the delivery boy with our stuff. Let's overhaul the outfit. I hope they'll get here with that burro, before dark. Where'll we put him, in the studio, heh?"

"Look here,"—said the artist a few minutes later, returning from a visit to the studio for something,—"this is what was the matter with Rutlidge. And you did it, old man. This is your key."

"What do you mean?" asked the other in confusion taking the key.

"Why, I found the studio door wide open, with your key in the lock. You must have been out there, just before we left this morning, and forgot to shut the door. Rutlidge probably noticed it when he was prowling about the place, and was trying to roast me for my carelessness."

Conrad Lagrange stared stupidly at the key in his hand. "Well I am damned," he muttered. Then added, in savage and—as it seemed to the artist—exaggerated wrath, "I'm a stupid, blundering, irresponsible old fool." Nor was he consoled when the painter innocently assured him that no harm had resulted from his carelessness.

That night, as the two men sat on the porch, watching the last of the light on the mountain tops, they heard again the cry of fear and pain that came from the little house hidden in the depths of the orange grove. Wonderingly they listened. Once more it came—filled with shuddering terror.

When the sound was not repeated, Conrad Lagrange thoughtfully knocked the ashes from his pipe. "Poor soul," he said. "Those scars did more than disfigure her beautiful face. I'll wager there's a sad story there, Aaron. It's strange how I am haunted by the impression that I ought to know her. But I can't make it come clear. Heigho,"—he added a moment later as if to free his mind from unpleasant thoughts,—"I'll be glad when we are safely up in the hills yonder. Do you know, old man, I feel as though we're getting away just in the nick of time. My back hair and the pricking of my thumbs warn me that your dearly beloved spooks are combining to put up some sort of a spooking job on us. I hope Yee Kee has a plentiful supply of joss-sticks to stand 'em off, if they get too busy while we are gone."

Aaron King laughed quietly in the dusk, as he returned "And I have a presentiment that those precious members of our household are preparing to accompany us to the hills. I feel in my bones that something is going to happen up there"—he pointed to the distant mountains, then added—"to me, at least. I feel as though I were about to bid myself good-by—if you know what I mean. I hope that donkey of ours isn't a psychic donkey, or, if he is, that he'll listen to reason and be content with his escorts of flesh and blood."

As he finished speaking, the quiet of the evening was broken by a lusty, "Hee-haw, hee-haw," in front of the house.

"There, I told you so!" ejaculated the painter.

Laughing, the two men followed Czar down the walk, in the dark, to receive the shaggy, long-eared companion for their wanderings.

As many a man has done—Aaron King had spoken, in jest, more truth than he knew.

Chapter XIV

In The Mountains

In the gray of the early morning, hours before the dwellers on Fairlands Heights thought of leaving their beds, Aaron King and Conrad Lagrange made ready for their going.

The burro, Croesus—so named by the novelist because, as the famous writer explained, "that ancient multi-millionaire, you know, really was an ass"—was to be entrusted with all the available worldly possessions of the little party. An arrangement—the more experienced man carefully pointed out—that, considering the chief characteristics of Croesus, was quite in accord with the customs of modern pilgrimages. Conrad Lagrange, himself, skillfully fixed the pack in place—adjusting the saddle with careful hand; accurately dividing the weight, with the blankets on top, and, over all, the canvas tarpaulin folded the proper size and neatly tucked in around the ends; and finally securing the whole with the, to the uninitiated, intricate and complicated diamond hitch. The order of their march, also, would place Croesus first; which position—the novelist, again, gravely explained, as he drew the cinches tight—is held by all who value good form, to be the donkey's proper place in the procession. As he watched his friend, the artist felt that, indeed, he was about to go far from the ways of life that he had always known.

When all was ready, the two men—dressed in flannels, corduroys, and high-laced, mountain boots—called good-by to Yee Kee, respectfully invited Croesus to proceed, and set out—with Czar, the fourth member of the party, flying here and there in such a whirlwind of good spirits that not a shred of his usual dignity was left. The sun was still below the mountain's crest, though the higher points were gilded with its light, when they turned their backs upon the city made by men, and set their faces toward the hills that bore in every ridge and peak and cliff and crag and canyon the signature of God.

As Conrad Lagrange said—they might have hired a wagon, or even an automobile, to take them and their goods to some mountain ranch where they would have had no trouble in securing a burro for their wanderings A team would have made the trip by noon. A machine would have set them down in Clear Creek Canyon before the sun could climb high enough to look over the canyon walls. "But that"— explained the novelist, as they trudged leisurely along between rows of palms that bordered the orange groves on either side of their road, and sensed the mystery that marks the birth of a new day—"but that is not a proper way to go to the mountains.

"The mountains"—he continued, with his eyes upon the distant heights—"are not seen by those who would visit them with a rattle and clatter and rush and roar—as one would visit the cities of men. They are to be seen only by those who have the grace to go quietly; who have the understanding to go thoughtfully; the heart to go lovingly; and the spirit to go worshipfully. They are to be approached, not in the manner of one going to a horse-race, or a circus, but in the mood of one about to enter a great cathedral; or, indeed, of one seeking admittance to the very throne-room of God. When going to the mountains, one should take time to feel them drawing near. They are never intimate with those who hurry. Mere sight-seers seldom see much of anything. If possible,"—insisted the speaker, smiling gravely upon his companion,—"one should always spend, at least, a full day in the approach. Before entering the immediate presence of the hills, one should first view them from a distance, seeing them from base to peak—in the glory of the day's beginning, as they watch the world awake; in the majesty of full noon, as they maintain their calm above the turmoil of the day's doing; and in the glory of the sun's departure, as it lights last their crests and peaks. And then, after such a day, one should sleep, one night, at their feet."

The artist listened with delight, as he always did when his friend spoke in those rare moods that revealed a nature so unknown to the world that had made him famous. When the novelist finished, the young man said gently, "And your words, my friend, are almost a direct quotation from that anonymous book which my mother so loved."

"Perhaps they are, Aaron"—admitted Conrad Lagrange—"perhaps they are."

So it was that they spent that day—in leisure approach—the patient Croesus, with his burden, always in the lead, and Czar, like a merry sprite, playing here and there. Several times they stopped to rest beside the road, while provident Croesus gathered a few mouthfuls of grass or weeds. Many times they halted to enjoy the scene that changed with every step.

Their road led always upward, with a gradual, easy grade; and by noon they had left the cultivated section of the lower valley for the higher, untilled lands. The dark, glossy-green of the orange and the lighter shining tints of the lemon groves, with the rich, satiny-gray tones of the olive-trees, were replaced now by the softer grays, greens, yellows, and browns of the chaparral. The air was no longer heavy with the perfume of roses and orange-blossoms, but came to their nostrils laden with the pungent odors of yerba santa and greasewood and sage. Looking back, they could see the valley—marked off by its roads into many squares of green, and dotted here and there by small towns and cities—stretching away toward the western ocean until it was lost in a gray-blue haze out of which the distant San Gabriels, beyond Cajon Pass, lifted into the clear sky above, like the shore-line of dreamland rising out of a dream sea. Before them, the San Bernardinos drew ever nearer and more intimate—silently inviting them; patiently, with a world old patience, bidding them come; in the majestic humbleness of their lofty spirit, offering themselves and the wealth of their teaching.

So they came, in the late afternoon, to that spot where the road for the first time crosses the alder and cottonwood bordered stream that, before it reaches the valley, is drawn from its natural course by the irrigation flumes and pipes.

The sound of the mountain waters leaping down their granite-bouldered way reached the men while they were yet some distance. Croesus pointed his long ears forward in burro anticipation—his experience telling him that the day's work was about to end. Czar was already ranging along the side of the creek—sending a colony of squirrels scampering to the tree tops, and a bevy of quail whirring to the chaparral in frightened flight. The artist greeted the waters with a schoolboy shout of gladness. Conrad Lagrange, with the smile and the voice of a man miraculously recreated, said quietly, "This is the place where we stop for the night."

Their camp was a simple matter. Croesus asked nothing but to be released from his burden—being quite capable of caring for himself. A wash in the clear, cold water of the brook; a simple meal, prepared by Conrad Lagrange over a small fire made of sticks gathered by the artist; their tarpaulin and blankets spread within sound of the music of the stream; a watching of the sun's glorious going down; a quiet pipe in the hush of the mysterious twilight; a "good night" in the soft darkness, when the myriad stars looked down upon the dull red glow of their camp-fire embers; with the guarding spirit of the mighty hills to give them peace—and they lay down to sleep at the mountain's feet.

There is no sleeping late in the morning when one sleeps in the open, under the stars. After breakfast, the artist received another lesson in packing, and they moved on toward the world that already seemed to dwarf that other world which they had left, by one day's walking, so far below. A heavy fog, rolling in from the ocean in the night, submerged the valley in its dull, gray depths—leaving to the eye no view but the view of the mountains before them, and forcing upon the artist's mind the weird impression that the life he had always known was a fantastically unreal dream.

And now,—as they approached,—the frowning entrance of Clear Creek Canyon grew more and more clearly defined. The higher peaks appeared to draw back and hide themselves behind the foothills, which—as the men came closer under their immediate slopes and walls—seemed to grow magically in height and bulk. A little before noon, they were in the rocky vestibule of the canyon. On either hand, the walls rose almost sheer, while their road, now, was but a narrow shelf under the overhanging cliffs, below which the white waters of the stream—cold from the snows so far above—tumbled impetuously over the boulders that obstructed their way—filling the hall-like gorge with tumultuous melody. Soon, the canyon narrowed to less than a stone's throw in width. The walls grew more grim and forbidding in their rocky nearness. And then they came to that point where, on either side, great cliffs, projecting, form the massive, rugged portals of the mountain's gate.

First seen, from a point where the road rounds a jutting corner on the extreme right, the projecting cliffs ahead appear as a blank wall of rock that forbids further progress. But, as the men moved forward,—the road swinging more toward the center of the gorge,—the cliffs seemed to draw apart, and, through the way thus opened, they saw the great canyon and the mountains beyond. It was as though a mighty, invisible hand rolled silently back those awful doors to give them entrance.

Abruptly, upon the inner side of the narrow passage the canyon widens to many times the width of the outer vestibule; and the road, crossing the creek, curves to the left; so that, looking back as they went, the two men saw the mighty doors closing again, behind them—as they had opened to let them in. It was as though that spirit sentinel, guarding the treasures of the hills, had jealously barred the way, that no one else from the world of men might follow.

Aaron King stopped. Drawing a deep breath, and removing his hat, he turned his face from that mountain wall, upward to the encircling pine-fringed ridges and towering peaks. He had, indeed, come far from the world that he had always known.

Conrad Lagrange, smiling, watched his friend, but spoke no word.

Clear Creek Canyon is a deep, narrow valley, some fifteen miles in length, and approaching a mile in its greatest width; lying between the main range of the San Bernardinos and the lower ridge of the Galenas. The lower end of the canyon is shut in by the sheer cliff walls, and by the rugged portals of the narrow entrance; the upper end is formed by the dividing ridge that separates the Clear Creek from the Cold Water country which opens out onto the Colorado Desert below San Gorgonio Pass and the peaks of the San Jacintos. Perhaps two miles above the entrance the canyon widens to its greatest width; and in this portion of the little valley,—which extends some five miles to where the walls again draw close,—located on the benches above the boulder-strewn wash of Clear Creek, are the homes of several mountain ranchers, and the Government Forest Ranger Station.

At the Ranger Station, they stopped—Conrad Lagrange wishing to greet the mountaineer official, whom he had learned to know on his former trip. But the Ranger was away somewhere, riding his lonely trails, and they did not tarry.

Just above the Station, they left the main road to follow the way that leads to the Morton Ranch in the mouth of Alder Canyon—a small side canyon leading steeply up to a low gap in the main range. Beyond Morton's, there is only a narrow trail. Three hundred yards above the ranch corral, where the road ends and the trail begins, the buildings of the mountaineer's home were lost to view. Except for the narrow winding path that they must follow single file, there was no sign of human life.

For three weeks, they knew no roads other than those lonely, mountain trails. At times, they walked under dark pines where the ground was thickly carpeted with the dead, brown needles and the air was redolent with the odor of the majestic trees; or made their camps at night, feeding their blazing fires with the pitchy knots and cones. At other times, they found their way through thickets of manzanita and buckthorn, along the mountain's flank; or, winding zigzag down some narrow canyon wall, made themselves at home under the slender, small-trunked alders; and added to the stores that Croesus packed, many a lusty trout from the tumbling, icy torrent. Again, high up on some wind-swept granite ridge or peak, where the pines were twisted and battered and torn by the warring elements, they looked far down upon the rolling sea of clouds that hid the world below; or, in the shelter of some mighty cliff, built their fires; and, when the night was clear, saw, miles away and below, the thousands of twinkling star-like lights of the world they had left behind. Or, again, they halted in some forest and hill encircled glen; where the lush grass in the cienaga grew almost as high as Croesus' back, and the lilies even higher; and where, through the dark green brakes, the timid deer come down to drink at the beginning of some mountain stream. At last, their wanderings carried them close under the snowy heights of San Gorgonio—the loftiest of all the peaks. That night, they camped at timber-line and in the morning,—leaving Croesus and the outfit, while it was still dark,—made their way to the top, in time to see the sun come up from under the edge of the world.

So they were received into the inner life of the mountains; so the spirit that dwells in that unmarred world whispered to them the secrets of its enduring strength and lofty peace.

From San Gorgonio, they followed the trail that leads down to upper Clear Creek—halting, one night, at Burnt Pine Camp on Laurel Creek, above the falls. Then—leaving the Laurel trail—they climbed over a spur of the main range, and so down the steep wall of the gorge to Lone Cabin on Fern Creek. The next day, they made their way on down to the floor of the main canyon—five miles above the point where they had left it at the beginning of their wanderings.

Crossing the canyon at the Clear Creek Power Company's intake, they took the company trail that follows the pipe-line along the southern wall. From the headwork to the reservoir two thousand feet above the power-house at the mouth of Clear Creek Canyon, this trail is cut in the steep side of the Galena range—overhanging the narrow valley below—nine beautiful miles of it. At Oak Knoll,—where a Government trail for the Forest Ranger zigzags down from the pipe-line to the wagon road below,—they halted.

Conrad Lagrange explained that there were three ways back to the world they had left, nearly a month before—the pipe-line trail to the reservoir and so down to the power-house and the Fairlands road; the Government trail from the pipe-line, over the Galenas to the valley on the other side; or, the Oak Knoll trail down to Clear Creek and out through the canyon gates—the way they had come.

"But," objected Aaron King, lazily,—from where he lay under a live-oak on the mountainside, a few feet above the trail,—"either route presupposes our wish to return to Fairlands."

The novelist laughed. "Listen to him, Czar,"—he said to the dog lying at his feet,—"listen to that painter-man. He doesn't want to go back to Fairlands any more than we do, does he?"

Rising, Czar looked at his master a moment, with slow waving tail, then turned inquiringly toward the artist.

"Well," said the young man, "what about it, old boy? Which trail shall we take? Or shall we take any of them?"

With a prodigious yawn,—as though to indicate that he wearied of their foolish indecision,—Czar turned, with a low "woof," toward the fourth member of the company, who was browsing along the edge of the trail. Whenever Czar was in doubt as to the wants of his human companions he always barked at the burro.

"He says, 'ask Croesus'," commented the artist.

"Good!" cried the older man, with another laugh. "Let's put it up to the financier and let him choose."

"Wait,"—said the artist, as the other turned toward the burro,—"don't be hasty—the occasion calls for solemn meditation and lofty discourse."

"Your pardon,"—returned the novelist,—"'tis so. I will orate." Carefully selecting a pebble in readiness to emphasize his remarks, he addressed the shaggy arbiter of their fate. "Sir Croesus, thy pack is lighter by many meals than when first thou didst set out from that land where we did rescue thee from the hands of thy tormenting trader; but thy responsibilities are weightier, many fold. Upon the wisdom of thy choice, now, great issue rests. Thou hast thy chance, O illustrious ass, to recompense the world, this day, for the many evils wrought by thy odious ancestor and by all his long-eared kin. Choose, now, the way thy benefactors' feet shall go; and see to it, Croesus, that thou dost choose wisely; or, by thy ears, we'll flay thy woolly hide and hang it on the mountainside—a warning to thy kind."

The well-thrown pebble struck that part of the burro's anatomy at which it was aimed; the dog barked; and Croesus—with an indignant jerk of his head, and a flirt of his tail—started forward. At the fork of the trail, he paused. The two men waited with breathless interest. With an air of accepting the responsibility placed upon him, the burro whirled and trotted down the narrow path that led to the floor of the canyon below. Laughing, the men followed—but far enough in the rear to permit their leader to choose his own way when they should reach the wagon road at the foot of the mountain wall. Without an instant's hesitation, Croesus turned down the road—quickening his pace, almost, into a trot.

"By George!" ejaculated the novelist, "he acts like he knew where he was going."

"He's taking you at your word," returned the artist. "Look at him go! Evidently, he's still under the inspiration of your oratory."

The burro had broken into a ridiculous, little gallop that caused the frying-pan and coffee-pot, lashed on the outside of the pack, to rattle merrily. Splashing through the creek, he disappeared in the dark shadow of a thicket of alders and willows, where the road crosses a tiny rivulet that flows from a spring a hundred yards above. Climbing out of this gloomy hollow, the road turns sharply to the left, and the men hurried on to overtake their four-footed guide before he should be too long out of their sight. Just at the top of the little rise, before rounding the turn, they stopped. A few feet to the right of the road, with his nose at an old gate, stood Croesus. Nor would he heed Czar's bark commanding him to go on.

On the other side of the fence, an old and long neglected apple orchard, a tumble-down log barn, and the wreck of a house with the fireplace and chimney standing stark and alone, told the story. The place was one of those old ranches, purchased by the Power Company for the water rights, and deserted by those who once had called it home. From the gate, ancient wagon tracks, overgrown with weeds, led somewhere around the edge of the orchard and were lost in the tangle of trees and brush on its lower side.

The two men looked at each other in laughing surprise. The burro, turning his head, gazed at them over his shoulder, inquiringly, as much as to say, "Well, what's the matter now? Why don't you come along?"

"When in doubt, ask Croesus," said the artist, gravely.

Conrad Lagrange calmly opened the gate.

Promptly, the burro trotted ahead. Following the ancient weed-grown tracks, he led them around the lower end of the orchard; crossed a little stream; and, turning again, climbed a gentle rise of open, grassy land behind the orchard; stopping at last, with an air of having accomplished his purpose, in a beautiful little grove of sycamore trees that bordered a small cienaga.

Completely hidden by the old orchard from the road in front, and backed by the foot of the mountain spur that here forms the northern wall of the little valley, the spot commanded a magnificent view of the encircling peaks and ridges. San Bernardino was almost above their heads. To the east, were the more rugged walls of the upper and narrower end of the canyon; in their front, the beautiful Oak Knoll, with the dark steeps and pine-fringed crest of the Galenas against the sky; while to the west, the blue peaks of the far San Gabriels showed above the lower spurs and foothills of the more immediate range. The foreground was filled in by the gentle slope leading down to the tiny stream at the edge of the old orchard and, a little to the left, by the cienaga—rich in the color of its tall marsh grass and reeds, gemmed with brilliant flowers of gold and scarlet, bordered by graceful willows, and screened from the eye of the chance traveler by the lattice of tangled orchard boughs.

Seated in the shade of the sycamores on the little knoll, the two friends enjoyed the beauty of the scene, and the charming seclusion of the lovely retreat; while Croesus stood patiently, as though waiting to be rewarded for his virtue, by the removal of his pack. Even Czar refrained from charging here and there, and lay down contentedly at their feet, with an air of having reached at last the place they had been seeking.

A few days later found them established in a comfortable camp; with tents and furniture and hammocks and books and the delighted Yee Kee to take care of them. It had been easy to secure permission from the neighboring rancher who leased the orchard from the Company. Conrad Lagrange, with the man and his big mountain wagon, had made a trip to town—returning the next day with Yee Kee and the outfit. He brought, also, things from the studio; for the artist declared that he would no longer be without the materials of his art.

The first day after the camp was built, the artist—declaring that he would settle the question, at once, as to whether Yee Kee could cook a trout as skillfully as the novelist—took rod and flies, and—leaving the famous author in a hammock, with Czar lying near—set out up the canyon. For perhaps two miles, the painter followed the creek—taking here and there from clear pool or swirling eddy a fish for his creel, and pausing often, as he went, to enjoy—in artist fashion—the beauties of the ever changing landscape.

The afternoon was almost gone when he finally turned back toward camp. He had been away, already longer than he intended; but still—as all fishermen will understand—he could not, on his way back down the stream, refrain from casting here and there over the pools that tempted him.

The sun was touching the crest of the mountains when he had made but little more than half the distance of his return. He had just sent his fly skillfully over a deep pool in the shadow of a granite boulder, for what he determined must be his last cast, when, startlingly clear and sweet, came the tones of a violin.

A master trout leaped. The hand of the unheeding fisherman felt the tug as the leader broke. Giving the victorious fish no thought, Aaron King slowly reeled in his line.

There was no mistaking the pure, vibrant tones of the music to which the man listened with amazed delight. It was the music of the, to him, unknown violinist who lived hidden in the orange grove next door to his studio home in Fairlands.

Chapter XV

The Forest Ranger's Story

Perhaps the motive that, in Fairlands, had restrained the artist from seeking to know his neighbor was without force in the mountains. Perhaps it was that, in the unconventional freedom of the hills, the man obeyed more readily his impulse. Aaron King did not stop to question. As though in answer to the call of that spirit which spoke in the tones of the violin, he moved in the direction from which the music came.

Climbing out of the bed of the stream to the bench that slopes hack—a quarter of a mile, perhaps—to the foot of the canyon wall, he found himself in an old road that, where it once crossed the creek, had been destroyed by the mountain floods. Wonderingly he followed the dimly marked track that led through the chaparral toward a thicket of cedars, from beyond which the music seemed to come. Where the road curved to find its way through the green barrier he paused—the musician, undoubtedly, now, was just beyond. Still acting upon the impulse of the moment, he cautiously parted the boughs and peered through into a little, open glade that was closed in on every side by the rank growth of the mountain vegetation, by the thicket of dark cedars and by tangled masses of wild rose-bushes. Opposite the spot where he stood, and half concealed by great sycamore trees, was a small, log house with a thread of blue smoke curling lazily from the chimney. The place was another of those old ranches that had been purchased by the Power Company and permitted to go back to the wilderness from which it had been won by some hardy settler. The little plot of open ground—well sodded with firm turf and short-cropped by roving cattle and deer—had evidently been, at one time, the front yard of the mountaineer's home. A little out from the porch, and in full view of the artist,—her graceful form outlined against the background of wild roses,—stood Sibyl Andrés with her violin.

As the girl played,—her winsome face upturned to the mountain heights and her body, lightly poised, swaying with the movement of her arm as easily as a willow bough,—she appeared, to the man hidden in the cedars, as some beautiful spirit of the woods and hills—a spirit that would vanish instantly if he should step from his hiding place. He was so close that he could see her blue eyes, wide and unmindful of her surroundings; her lips, curved in an unconscious smile; and her cheeks, flushed with emotion under their warm brown tint—as she appeared to listen for the music that she, in turn,—seemingly with no effort of her will,—gave forth again in the tones of the instrument under her chin.

Aaron King was moved by the beauty of the picture as he had never been stirred before. The peculiar charm of the music; the loveliness of the girl herself; the setting of the scene in the little glade with its wild roses, giant sycamores, dark cedars, and encircling mountain walls, all in the soft mystery of the twilight's beginning; and, withal, the unexpectedness of the vision—combined to make an impression upon the artist's mind that would endure for many years.

Suddenly, as he watched, the music ceased. The girl lowered her violin, and, with a low laugh, said to some one on the porch—concealed from the painter by the trunk of a sycamore—"O Myra, I want to dance. I can't keep still. I'm so glad, glad to be home again—to see old 'San Berdo' and 'Gray Back' and all the rest of them up there!" She stretched out her arms as if in answer to a welcome from the hills. Then, whirling quickly, she gave the violin to her companion on the porch. "Play, Myra; please, dear, play."

At her word, the music of the violin began again—coming now, from behind the trunk of the sycamore. In the hands of the unseen musician, the instrument laughed and sang a song of joyous abandonment— of freedom and rejoicing—of happiness and love—while in perfect harmony with the spirit and the rhythm of the melody, the girl danced upon the firm, green carpet of grass. Here and there, to and fro, about the little glade shut in from the world by its walls of living green, she tripped and whirled in unstudied grace—lightly as if winged—unconscious as the wild creatures that play in the depths of the woods—wayward as the zephyr that trips along the mountainside.

It was a spontaneous expression of her spiritual and physical exaltation and was as natural as the laughter in her voice or the flush upon her cheeks. It was a dance that was like no dance that Aaron King had ever seen.

The artist—watching through the screen of cedar boughs beside the old wagon road and scarcely daring to breathe lest the beautiful vision should vanish—forgot his position—forgot what he was doing. Fascinated by the scene to which he had been led, so unexpectedly by the music he had so often heard while at work in his studio, he was unmindful of the rude part he was playing. He was brought suddenly to himself by a heavy hand upon his shoulder. As he straightened, the hand whirled him half around and he found himself looking into a face that was tanned and seamed by many years in the open.

The man who had so unceremoniously commanded the artist's attention stood a little above six feet in height, and was of that deep-chested, lean, but full-muscled build that so often marks the mountain bred. He wore no coat. At his hip, a heavy Colt revolver hung in its worn holster from a full, loosely buckled, cartridge belt. Upon his unbuttoned vest was the shield of the United States Forest Service. From under the brim of his slouch hat, he gazed at Aaron King questioningly—in angry disapproval.

Instinctively, neither of the men spoke. A word would have been heard the other side of the cedars. With a gesture commanding the artist to follow, the Ranger quietly, withdrew along the wagon road toward the creek.

When they were at a distance where their voices would not reach the girl in the glade, the Ranger said with angry abruptness, "Now, sir, perhaps you will tell me who you are and what you mean by spying upon a couple of women, like that."

The other could not conceal his embarrassment. "I don't blame you for calling me to account," he said. "If it were me—if our positions were reversed I mean—I should kick you down into the creek there."

The cold, blue eyes—that had been measuring the painter so shrewdly—twinkled with a hint of humor. "You do look like a gentleman, you know," the officer said,—as if excusing himself for not following the artist's suggestion. "But, all the same, you must explain. Who are you?"

"That part is easy, at least," returned the other. "Though the circumstance of our meeting is a temptation to lie."

"Which would do you no good, and might lead to unpleasant complications," retorted the Ranger, sharply.

The man under question, still embarrassed, laughed shortly, as he returned, "I really was not thinking of it seriously. My name is Aaron King. I am an artist. You are Mr. Oakley, I suppose."

The officer nodded—beginning to smile. "Yes, I am Brian Oakley."

The artist continued, "A month ago, Conrad Lagrange and I came into the mountains for an outing. We stopped at the Station, but there was no one at home. Most of the time, we have been just roaming around. Now, we are camped down there, back of that old apple orchard."

The Ranger broke into a laugh. "Mrs. Oakley was visiting friends up the canyon, the day you came in; but Morton told me. I've crossed your trail a dozen times, and sighted you nearly as many; but I was always too busy to go to you. I knew Lagrange didn't need any attention, you see; so I just figured on meeting up with you somewhere by accident like—about meal time, mebbe." He laughed again. "The accident part worked out all right." He paused, still laughing—enjoying the artist's discomfiture; then ended with a curious—"What in thunder were you sneaking around in the brush like that for, anyway? Those women won't bite."

Aaron King explained how he had heard the music while fishing; and how, following the sound, he had acted upon an impulse to catch a glimpse of the unknown musician before revealing himself; and then, in his interest, had forgotten that he was playing the part of a spy—until so rudely aroused by the hand of the Ranger.

Brian Oakley chuckled; "If I'd acted upon impulse when I first saw you peeking through those cedars, you would have been more surprised than you were. But while I was sneaking up on you I noticed your get-up—with your creel and rod—and figured how you might have come there. So I thought I would go a little slow."

"And you wear rather heavy boots too," said the artist suggestively. Then, more at ease, he joined in the laugh at himself.

"Catch any fish?" asked the Ranger—lifting the cover of the creel. "Whee!" as he saw the contents. "That's bully! And I'm hungry as a she wolf too! Been in the saddle since sunup without a bite. What do you say if I make that long deferred social call upon you and Lagrange this evening?"

"I say, good! Mr. Oakley," returned the artist, heartily. "I guess you know what Lagrange will say."

"You bet I do." He whistled—a low, birdlike note. In answer, a beautiful, chestnut saddle-horse came out of the chaparral, where it had not been seen by the painter. "We're going, Max," said the officer, in a matter-of-fact way. And, as the two men set out, the horse followed, with a business-like air that brought a word of admiring comment from the artist.

That Aaron King had won the approval of the Ranger was evidenced by the mountaineer's inviting himself to supper the camp in the sycamores. The fact that the officer considerately told Conrad Lagrange only that he had met the artist with his creel full of trout, and so had been tempted to accompany him, won the enduring gratitude of the young man. Thus the circumstances of their meeting introduced each to the other, with recommendations of peculiar value, and marked the beginning of a genuine and lasting friendship. But, while, out of delicate regard for the artist's feelings, he refrained from relating the—to the young man—embarrassing incident, Brian Oakley could not resist making, at every opportunity, sly references to their meeting—for the painter's benefit and his own amusement. Thus it happened that, after supper, as they sat with their pipes, the talk turned upon Sibyl Andrés and the woman with the disfigured face.

The Ranger, to tease the artist, had remarked casually,—after complimenting them upon the location of their camp,—"And you've got some mighty nice neighbors, less than a mile above too."

"Neighbors!" ejaculated Conrad Lagrange—in a tone that left no doubt as to his sentiment in the matter.

The others laughed; while the officer said, "Oh, I know how you feel! You think you don't want anybody poaching on your preserves. You're up here in the hills to get away from people, and all that. But you don't need to be uneasy. You won't even see these folks—unless you sneak up on them." He stole a look at the artist, and chuckled maliciously as the painter covertly shook his fist at him. "You may hear them though."

"Which would probably be as bad," retorted the novelist, gruffly.

"Oh, I don't know!" returned the other. "You might be able to stand it. I don't reckon you would object to a little music now and then, would you?—real music, I mean."

"So our neighbors are musical, are they?" The novelist seemed slightly interested.

"Sibyl Andrés is the most accomplished violinist I have ever heard," said the Ranger. "And I haven't always lived in these mountains, you know. As for Myra Willard—well—she taught Sibyl—though she doesn't pretend to equal her now."

Conrad Lagrange was interested, now, in earnest He turned to the artist, eagerly—but with caution—"Do you suppose it could be our neighbors in the orange grove, Aaron?"

Brian Oakley watched them with quiet amusement.

"I know it is," returned the artist.

"You know it is!" ejaculated the other.

"Sure—I heard the violin this afternoon. While I was fishing," he added hastily, when the Ranger laughed.

The novelist commented savagely, "Seems to me you're mighty careful about keeping your news to yourself!"

This brought another burst of merriment from the mountaineer.

When the two men had explained to the Ranger about the music in the orange grove, Conrad Lagrange related how they had first heard that cry in the night; and how, when they had gone to the neighboring house, they had seen the woman of the disfigured face standing in the doorway.

"It was Miss Willard who cried out," said Brian Oakley, quietly. "She dreams, sometimes, of the accident—or whatever it was—that left her with those scars—at least, that's what I think it is. Certainly it's no ordinary dream that would make a woman cry like that. The first time I heard her—the first time that she ever did it, in fact—she and Sibyl were stopping over night at my house. It was three years ago. Jim Rutlidge had just come West, on his first trip, and was up in the hills on a hunt. He happened along about sundown, and when he stepped into the room and Myra saw him, I thought she would faint. He looked like some one she had known—she said. And that night she gave that horrible cry. Lord! but it threw a fright into me. My wife didn't get over being nervous, for a week. Myra explained that she had dreamed—but that's all she would say. I figured that being upset by Rutlidge's reminding her of some one she had known started her mind to going on the past—and then she dreamed of whatever it was that gave her those scars."

"You have known Miss Willard a long time, haven't you, Brian?" asked Conrad Lagrange, with the freedom of an old comrade—for men may grow closer together in one short season in the mountains than in years of meeting daily in the city.

"I've known her ever since she came into the hills. That was the year Sibyl was born. All that anybody knows is what has happened since. Sibyl's mother, even—a month before she died—told me that Myra's history, before she came to them, was as unknown to her as it was the day she stopped at their door."

"I can't get over the feeling that I ought to know her—that I have seen her somewhere, years ago," said the novelist, by way of explaining his interest.

"Then it was before she got those scars," returned the Ranger. "No one could ever forget her face as it is now."

"At the same time," commented the artist, "the scars would prevent your identifying her if she received them after you had known her."

"All the same," said Conrad Lagrange,—as though his mind was bothered by his inability to establish some incident in his memory,—"I'll place her yet. Do you mind, Brian, telling us what you do know of her?"

"Why, not at all," returned the officer. "The story is anybody's property. Its being so well known is probably the reason you didn't hear it when you were up here before.

"Sibyl's father and mother were here in the mountains when I came. They lived up there at the old place where Myra and Sibyl are camping now, and I never expect to meet finer people—either in this world or the next. For twenty years I knew them intimately. Will Andrés was as true and square and white a man as ever lived and Nelly was just as good a woman as he was a man. They and my wife and I were more like brothers and sisters than most folks who are actually blood kin.

"One day, along toward sundown, about a month before Sibyl was born, Nelly heard the dogs barking and went to see what was up. There stood Myra Willard at the gate—like she'd dropped out of the sky. Where she came from God only knows—except that she'd walked from some station on the railroad over toward the pass. She was just about all in; and, of course, Nelly had her into the house and was fixing her up in no time. She wanted to work, but admitted that she had never done much housework. She said, straight out, that they should never know more about her than they knew, then; but insisted that she was not a bad woman. At first, Will and I were against it for, of course, it was easy to see that she was trying to get away from something. But the women—Nelly and my wife—somehow, believed in her, and—with the baby due to arrive in a month and any kind of help hard to get—they carried the day. Well, sir, she made good. If twenty years acquaintance goes for anything, she's one of God's own kind, and I don't care a damn what her history is.

"We soon saw that she was educated and refined, and—as you can see for yourself—she must have been remarkably beautiful before she got so disfigured. When the baby was born, she just took the little one into her poor, broken heart like it had been her own, until Sibyl hardly knew which was her own mother. When the girl was old enough for school, Myra begged Will and Nelly to let her teach the child. She was always sending for books and it was about that time that she sent for a violin. The girl took to music like a bird. And—well—that's the way Sibyl was raised. She's got all the education that the best of them have—even to French and Italian and German—and she's missed some things that the schools teach outside of their text-books. She has a library—given to her mostly by Myra, a book at a time—that represents the best of the world's best writers. You know what her music is. But, hell!"—the Ranger interrupted himself with an apologetic laugh—"I'm supposed to be talking about Myra Willard. I don't know as I'm so far off, either, because what Sibyl is—aside from her natural inheritance from Will and Nelly—Myra has made her.

"When Will was killed by those Mexican outlaws,—which is a story in itself,—Nelly sold the ranch to the Power Company, and bought an orange grove in Fairlands—which was the thing for her to do, as she and Myra could handle that sort of property, and the ranch had to go, anyway. Before Nelly died, she and I talked things over, and she put everything in Myra's hands, in trust for the girl. Later, Myra sold the grove and the house where you men live, now, and bought the little place next door—putting the rest of the money into gilt-edged securities in Sibyl's name; which insures the girl against want, for years to come. Sibyl helps out their income with her music. And that's the story, boys, except that they come up here into the mountains, every summer, to spend a month or so in the old home place."

The Ranger rose to go.

"But do you think it is safe for those women to stay up there alone?" asked Aaron King.

Brian Oakley laughed. "Safe! You don't know Myra Willard! Sibyl, herself, can pick a squirrel out of the tallest pine in the mountains with her six-shooter. Will and I taught her all we knew, as she grew up. Besides, you see, I drop in every day or so, to see that they're all right." He laughed meaningly as he added,—to Conrad Lagrange for the artist's benefit,—"I'm going to tell them, though, that Sibyl must be careful how she goes dancing around these hills—now that she has such distinguished but irresponsible neighbors."

He whistled—and the chestnut horse was at his side before the echo of their laughter died away.

With a "so-long," the Ranger rode away into the night.

Chapter XVI

When the Canyon Gates Are Shut

If Aaron King had questioned what it was that had held him in the cedar thicket until Brian Oakley's heavy hand broke the spell, he would probably have answered that it was his artistic appreciation of the beautiful scene. But—deep down in the man's inner consciousness—there was a still, small voice—declaring, with an insistency not to be denied, that—for him—there was a something in that picture that was not to be put into the vernacular of his profession.

Had he acted without his habitual self-control, the day following the Ranger's visit, he would, again, have gone fishing—up Clear Creek—at least, to the pool where that master trout had broken his leader. But he did not. Instead, he roamed aimlessly about the vicinity of the camp—explored the sycamore grove; climbed a little way up the mountain spur, and down again; circled the cienaga; and so came, finally, to the ruins of the house and barn on the creek side of the orchard.

Not far from the lonely fireplace with its naked chimney, a little, old gate of split palings, in an ancient tumble-down fence, under a great mistletoe-hung oak, at the top of a bank—attracted his careless attention. From the gate, he saw what once had been a path leading down the bank to a spring, where the tiny streamlet that crossed the road a hundred yards away, on its course to Clear Creek, began. Pushing open the gate that sagged dejectedly from its leaning post, the artist went down the path, and found himself in a charming nook—shut in on every side by the forest vegetation that, watered by the spring, grew rank and dense.

For a space on the gate side of the spring, the sod was firm and smooth—with a gray granite boulder in the center of the little glade, and, here and there, wild rose-bushes and the slender, gray trunks of alder trees breaking through. From the higher branches of the alders that shut out the sky with their dainty, silvery-green leaves, hung—with many a graceful loop and knot—ropes of wild grape-vine and curtains of virgin's-bower. Along the bank below the old fence, the wild blackberries disputed possession with the roses; while the little stream was mottled with the tender green of watercress and bordered with moss and fragrant mint. Above the arroyo willows, on the farther side of the glade, Oak Knoll, with bits of the pine-clad Galenas, could be glimpsed; but on the orchard side, the vine-dressed bank with the old gate under the mistletoe oak shut out the view. Through the screen of alder and grape and willow and virgin's-bower the sunlight fell, as through the delicate traceries of a cathedral window. The bright waters of the spring, softly held by the green sod, crept away under the living wall, without a sound; but the deep murmur of the distant, larger stream, reached the place like the low tones of some great organ. A few regularly placed stones, where once had stood the family spring-house; with the names, initials, hearts and dates carved upon the smooth bark of the alders—now grown over and almost obliterated—seemed to fill the spot with ghostly memories.

All that afternoon, the artist remained in the little retreat. The next day, equipped with easel, canvas and paint-box, he went again to the glade—determined to make a picture of the charming scene.

For a month, now, uninterrupted by the distractions of social obligations or the like, Aaron King had been subjected to influences that had aroused the creative passion of his artist soul to its highest pitch. With his genius clamoring for expression, he had denied himself the medium that was his natural language. Forbidding his friend to accompany him, he worked now in the spring glade with a delight— with an ecstasy—that he had seldom, before, felt. And Conrad Lagrange, wisely, was content to let him go uninterrupted.

As the hours of each day passed, the artist became more and more engrossed with his art. His spirit sang with the joy of receiving the loveliness of the scene before him, of making it his own, and of giving it forth again—a literal part of himself. The memories suggested by the stones of the spring-house foundation and the old carvings on the trees; the sunlight, falling so softly into the hushed seclusion of the glade, as through the traceried windows of a church; and the deep organ-tones of the distant creek; all served to give to the spot the religious atmosphere of a sanctuary; while the artist's abandonment in his work was little short of devotion.

It was the third afternoon, when the painter became conscious that he had been hearing for some time—he could not have said how long—a low-sung melody—so blending with the organ-tones of the mountain stream that it seemed to come out of the music of the tumbling waters.

With his brush poised between palette and canvas, the artist paused,—turning his head to listen,—half inclined to the belief that his fancy was tricking him. But no; the singer was coming nearer; the melody was growing more distinct; but still the voice was in perfect harmony with the deep-toned accompaniment of the distant creek.

Then he saw her. Dressed in soft brown that blended subtly with the green of the willows, the gray of the alder trunks, the russet of rose and blackberry-bush, and the umber of the swinging grape-vines—in the flickering sunshine, the soft changing half-lights, and deep shadows—she appeared to grow out of the scene itself; even as her low-sung melody grew out of the organ-sound of the waters.

To get the effect that satisfied him best, the painter had placed his easel a little back from the grassy, open spot. Seated as he was, on a low camp-stool, among the bushes, he would not have been easily observed—even by eyes trained to the quickness of vision that belongs to those reared in the woods and hills. As the girl drew closer, he saw that she carried a basket on her arm, and that she was picking the wild blackberries that grew in such luscious profusion in the rich, well watered ground at the foot of the sheltering bank. Unconscious of any listener, as she gathered the fruit of Nature's offering, she sang to the accompaniment of Nature's music, with the artless freedom of a wild thing unafraid in its native haunts.

The man kept very still. Presently, when the girl had moved so that he could not see her, he turned to his canvas as if, again, absorbed in his work—but hearing still, behind him, the low-voiced melody of her song.

Then the music ceased; not abruptly, but dying away softly—losing itself, again, in the organ-tones of the distant waters, as it had come. For a while, the artist worked on; not daring to take his eyes from his picture; but feeling, in every tingling nerve of him, that she was there. At last, as if compelled, he abruptly turned his head—and looked straight into her face.

The man had been, apparently, so absorbed in his work, when first the girl caught sight of him, that she had scarcely been startled. When she had ceased her song, and he, still, had not looked around; drawn by her interest in the picture, she had softly approached until she was standing quite close. Her lips were slightly parted, her face was flushed, and her eyes were shining with delight and excited pleasure, as she stood leaning forward, her basket on her arm. So interested was she in the painting, that she seemed to have quite forgotten the painter, and was not in the least embarrassed when he so suddenly looked directly into her face.

"It is beautiful," she said, as though in answer to his question. And no one—hearing her, and watching her face as she spoke—could have doubted her sincerity. "It is so true, so—so"—she searched for a word, and smiled in triumph when she found it—"so right—so beautifully right. It—it makes me feel as—as I feel when I am at church—and the organ plays soft and low, and the light comes slanting through the window, and some one reads those beautiful words, 'The Lord is in his holy temple; let all the earth keep silence before him'."

"Why!" exclaimed the artist, "that is exactly what I wanted it to say. When I saw this place, and heard the waters over there, like a great organ; and saw how the sunshine falls through the trees; I felt as you say, and I am trying to paint the picture so that those who see it will feel that way too."

Her face was aglow with enthusiastic understanding as she cried eagerly, "Oh, I know! I know! I'm like that with my music! When I look at the mountains sometimes—or at the trees and flowers, or hear the waters sing, or the winds call—I—I get so full and so—so kind of choked up inside that it hurts; and I feel as though I must try to tell it—and then I take my violin and try and try to make the music say what I feel. I never can though—not altogether. But you have made your picture say what you feel. That's what makes it so right, isn't it? They said in Fairlands that you were a great artist, and I understand why, now. It must be wonderful to put what you see and feel into a picture like that—where nothing can ever change or spoil it."

Aaron King laughed with boyish embarrassment. "Oh, but I'm not a great artist, you know. I am scarcely known at all."

She looked at him with her great, blue eyes sincerely troubled. "And must one be known—to be great?" she asked. "Might not an artist be great and still be unknown? Or, might not one who was really very, very"—again she seemed to search for a word and as she found it, smiled—"very small, be known all over the world? The newspapers make some really bad people famous, sometimes, don't they? No, no, you are joking. You do not really think that being known to the world and greatness are the same."

The man, studying her closely, saw that she was speaking her thoughts as openly as a child. Experimentally, he said, "If putting what you feel into your work is greatness, then you are a great artist, for your music does make one feel as though it came from the mountains, themselves."

She was frankly pleased, and cried intimately, "Oh! do you like my music? I so wanted you to."

It did not occur to her to ask when he had heard her music. It did not occur to him to explain. They, neither of them, thought to remember that they had not been introduced. They really should have pretended that they did not know each other.

"Sometimes," she continued with winsome confidence, "I think, myself, that I am really a great violinist—and then, again,"—she added wistfully,—"I know that I am not. But I am sure that I wouldn't like to be famous, at all."

He laughed. "Fame doesn't seem to matter so much, does it; when one is up here in the hills and the canyon gates are closed."

She echoed his laughter with quick delight. "Did you see that? Did you see those great doors open to let you in, and then close again behind you as if to shut the world outside? But of course you would. Any one who could do that"—she pointed to the canvas—"would not fail to see the canyon gates." With her eyes again upon the picture, she seemed once more to forget the presence of the painter.

Watching her face,—that betrayed her every passing thought and emotion as an untroubled pool mirrors the flowers that grow on its banks or the song-bird that pauses to drink,—the artist—to change her mood—said, "You love the mountains, don't you?"

She turned her face toward him, again, as she answered simply, "Yes, I love the mountains."

"If you were a painter,"—he smiled,—"you would paint them, wouldn't you?"

"I don't know that I would,"—she answered thoughtfully,—"but I would try to get the mountains into my picture, whatever it was. I wonder if you know what I mean?"

"Yes," he answered, "I think I know what you mean; and it is a beautiful thought. You wouldn't paint portraits, would you?"

"I don't think I could," she answered. "It seems to me it would be so hard to get the mountains into a portrait of just anybody. An artist—a great artist, I mean—must make his picture right, mustn't he? And if his picture was a portrait of some one who wasn't very good, and he made it right; he wouldn't be liked very well, would he? No, I don't think I would paint portraits—unless I could paint just the people who would want me to make my picture right."

Aaron King's face flushed at the words that were spoken so artlessly; and he looked at her keenly. But the girl was wholly innocent of any purpose other than to express her thoughts. She did not dream of the force with which her simple words had gone home.

"You love the mountains, too, don't you?" she asked suddenly.

"Yes," he answered, "I love the mountains. I am learning to love them more and more. But I fear I don't know them as well as you do."

"I was born up here," she said, "and lived here until a few years ago. I think, sometimes, that the mountains almost talk to me."

"I wonder if you would help me to know the mountains as you know them," he asked eagerly.

She drew a little back from him, but did not answer.

"We are neighbors, you see," he continued smiling. "I heard your violin, the other evening, when I was fishing up the creek, near where you live; and so I know it is you who live next door to us in the orange grove. Mr. Lagrange and I are camped just over there back of the orchard. May we not be friends? Won't you help me to know your mountains?"

"I know about you," she said. "Brian Oakley told us that you and Mr. Lagrange were camped down here. Mr. Lagrange said that you are a good man; Brian Oakley says that you are too—are you?"

The artist flushed. In his embarrassment, he did not note the significance of her reference to the novelist. "At least," he said gently, "I am not a very bad man."

A smile broke over her face—her mood changing as quickly as the sunlight breaks through a cloud. "I know you are not"—she said—"a bad man wouldn't have wanted to paint this place as you have painted it."

She turned to go.

"But wait!" he cried, "you haven't told me—will you teach me to know your mountains as you know them?"

"I'm sure I cannot say," she answered smiling, as she moved away.

"But at least, we will meet again," he urged.

She laughed gaily, "Why not? The mountains are for you as well as for me; and though the hills are so big, the trails are narrow, and the passes very few."

With another laugh, she slipped away—her brown dress, that, in the shifty lights under the thick foliage, so harmonized with the colors of bush and vine and tree and rock, being so quickly lost to the artist's eye that she seemed almost to vanish into the scene before him.

But presently, from beyond the willow wall, he heard her voice again—singing to the accompaniment of the mountain stream. Softly, the melody died away in the distance—losing itself, at last, in the deeper organ-tones of the mountain waters.

For some minutes, the artist stood listening—thinking he heard it still.

Aaron King did not, that night, tell Conrad Lagrange of his adventure in the spring glade.

Chapter XVII

Confessions in the Spring Glade

All the next day, while he worked upon his picture in the glade, Aaron King listened for that voice in the organ-like music of the distant waters. Many times, he turned to search the flickering light and shade of the undergrowth, behind him, for a glimpse of the girl's brown dress and winsome face.

The next day she came.

The artist had been looking long at a splash of sunlight that fell upon the gray granite boulder which was set in the green turf, and had turned to his canvas for—it seemed to him—only an instant. When he looked again at the boulder, she was standing there—had, apparently, been standing there for some time, waiting with smiling lips and laughing eyes for him to see her.

A light creel hung by its webbed strap from her shoulder; in her hand, she carried a slender fly rod of good workmanship. Dressed in soft brown, with short skirts and high laced boots, and her wavy hair tucked under a wide, felt hat; with her blue eyes shining with fun, and her warmly tinted skin glowing with healthful exercise; she appeared—to the artist—more as some mythical spirit of the mountains, than as a maiden of flesh and blood. The manner of her coming, too, heightened the impression. He had heard no sound of her approach—no step, no rustle of the underbrush. He had seen no movement among the bushes—no parting of the willows in the wall of green. There had been no hint of her nearness. He could not even guess the direction from which she had come.

At first, he could scarce believe his eyes, and sat motionless in his surprise. Then her merry laugh rang out—breaking the spell.

Springing from his seat, he went forward. "Are you a spirit?" he cried. "You must be something unreal, you know—the way you appear and disappear. The last time, you came out of the music of the waters, and went again the same way. To-day, you come out of the air, or the trees, or, perhaps, that gray boulder that is giving me such trouble."

Laughing, she answered, "My father and Brian Oakley taught me. If you will watch the wild things in the woods, you can learn to do it too. I am no more a spirit than the cougar, when it stalks a rabbit in the chaparral; or a mink, as it slips among the rocks along the creek; or a fawn, when it crouches to hide in the underbrush."

"You have been fishing?" he asked.

She laughed mockingly, "You are so observing! I think you might have taken that for granted, and asked what luck."

"I believe I might almost take that for granted too," he returned.

"I took a few," she said carelessly. Then, with a charming air of authority—"And now, you must go back to your work. I shall vanish instantly, if you waste another moment's time because I am here."

"But I want to talk," he protested. "I have been working hard since noon."

"Of course you have," she retorted. "But presently the light will change again, and you won't be able to do any more to-day; so you must keep busy while you can."

"And you won't vanish—if I go on with my work?" he asked doubtfully. She was smiling at him with such a mischievous air, that he feared, if he turned away, she would disappear.

She laughed aloud; "Not if you work," she said. "But if you stop—I'm gone."

As she spoke, she went toward his easel, and, resting her fly rod carefully against the trunk of a near-by alder, slipped the creel from her shoulder, placing the basket on the ground with her hat. Then, while the painter watched her, she stood silently looking at the picture. Presently, she faced him, and, with an impulsive stamp of her foot, said, "Why don't you work? How can you waste your time and this light, looking at me? I shall go, if you don't come back to your picture, this minute."

With a laugh, he obeyed.

For a moment, she watched him; then turned away; and he heard her moving about, down by the tiny stream, where it disappeared under the willows.

Once, he paused and turned to look in her direction "What are you up to, now?" he said.

"I shall be up to leaving you,"—she retorted,—"if you look around, again."

He promptly turned once more to his picture.

Soon, she came back, and seated herself beside her creel and rod, where she could see the picture under the artist's brush. "Does it bother, if I watch?" she asked softly.

"No, indeed," he answered. "It helps—that is, it helps when it is you who watch." Which—to the painter's secret amazement—was a literal truth. The gray rock with the splash of sunshine that would not come right, ceased to trouble him, now. Stimulated by her presence, he worked with a freedom and a sureness that was a delight.

When he could not refrain from looking in her direction, he saw that she was bending, with busy hands, over some willow twigs in her lap. "What in the world are you doing?" he asked curiously.

"You are not supposed to know that I am doing anything," she retorted. "You have been peeking again."

"You were so still—I feared you had vanished," he laughed. "If you'll keep talking to me, I'll know you are there, and will be good."

"Sure it won't bother?"

"Sure," he answered.

"Well, then, you talk to me, and I'll answer."

"I have a confession to make," he said, carefully studying the gray tones of the alder trunk beyond the gray boulder.

"A confession?"

"Yes, I want to get it over—so it won't bother me."

"Something about me?"

"Yes."

"Why, that's what I am trying so hard to make you keep your eyes on your work for—because I have to make a confession to you."

"To me?"

"Yes—don't look around, please."

"But what under the sun can you have to confess to me?"

"You started yours first," she answered. "Go on. Maybe it will make it easier for me."

Studiously keeping his eyes upon his canvas, he told her how he had watched her from the cedar thicket. When he had finished,—and she was silent,—he thought that she was angry, and turned about—expecting to see her gathering up her things to go.

She was struggling to suppress her laughter. At the look of surprise on his face, she burst forth in such a gale of merriment that the little glade was filled with the music of her glee; while, in spite of himself, the painter joined.

"Oh!" she cried, "but that is funny! I am glad, glad!"

"Now, what do you mean by that?" he demanded.

"Why—why—that's exactly what I was trying to get courage enough to confess to you!" she gasped. And then she told him how she had spied upon him from the arbor in the rose garden; and how, in his absence, she had visited his studio.

"But how in the world did you get in? The place was always locked, when I was away."

"Oh," she said quaintly, "there was a good genie who let me in through the keyhole. I didn't meddle with anything, you know—I just looked at the beautiful room where you work. And I didn't glance, even, at the picture on the easel. The genie told me you wouldn't like that. I would not have drawn the curtain anyway, even if I hadn't been told. At least, I don't think I would—but perhaps I might—I can't always tell what I'm going to do, you know."

Suddenly, the artist remembered finding the studio door open with Conrad Lagrange's key in the lock, and how the novelist had berated himself with such exaggerated vehemence; and, in a flash, came the thought of James Rutlidge's visit, that afternoon, and of his strange manner and insinuating remarks.

"I think I know the name of your good genie," said the painter, facing the girl, seriously. "But tell me, did no one disturb you while you were in the studio?"

Her cheeks colored painfully, and all the laughter was gone from her voice as she replied, "I didn't want you to know that part."

"But I must know," he insisted gravely.

"Yes," she said, "Mr. Rutlidge found me there; and I ran away through the garden. I don't like him. He frightens me. Please, is it necessary for us to talk about it any more? I had to make my confession of course, but must we talk about that part?"

"No," he answered, "we need not talk about it. It was necessary for me to know; but we will never mention that part, again. When we are back in the orange groves, you shall come to the rose garden and to the studio, as often as you like; your good genie and I will see to it that you are not disturbed—by any one."

Her face brightened at his words. "And do you really like for me to make music for you—as Mr. Lagrange says you do?"

"I can't begin to tell you how much I like it," he answered smiling.

"And it doesn't bother you in your work?"

"It helps me," he declared—thinking of that portrait of Mrs. Taine.

"Oh, I am glad, glad!" she cried. "I wanted it to help. It was for that I played."

"You played to help me?" he asked wonderingly.

She nodded. "I thought it might—if I could get enough of the mountains into my music, you know."

"And will you dance for me, sometimes too?" he asked.

She shook her head. "I cannot tell about that. You see, I only dance when I must—when the music, somehow, doesn't seem quite enough. When I—when I"—she searched for a word, then finished abruptly—"oh, I can't tell you about it—it's just something you feel—there are no words for it. When I first come to the mountains,—after living in Fairlands all winter,—I always dance—the mountains feel so big and strong. And sometimes I dance in the moonlight—when it feels so soft and light and clean; or in the twilight—when it's so still, and the air is so—so full of the day that has come home to rest and sleep; and sometimes when I am away up under the big pines and the wind, from off the mountain tops, under the sky, sings through the dark branches."

"But don't you ever dance to please your friends?"

"Oh, no—I don't dance to please any one—only just when it's for myself—when nothing else will do— when I must. Of course, sometimes, Myra or Brian Oakley or Mrs. Oakley are with me—but they don't matter, you know. They are so much a part of me that I don't mind."

"I wonder if you will ever dance for me?"

Again, she shook her head. "I don't think so. How could I? You see, you are not like anybody that I have ever known."

"But I saw you the other evening, you remember."

"Yes, but I didn't know you were there. If I had known, I wouldn't have danced."

All the while—as she talked—her fingers had been busy with the slender, willow branches. "And now"—she said, abruptly changing the subject, and smiling as she spoke—"and now, you must turn back to your work."

"But the light is not right," he protested.

"Never mind, you must pretend that it is," she retorted. "Can't you pretend?"

To humor her, he obeyed, laughing.

"You may look, now," she said, a minute later.

He turned to see her standing close beside him, holding out a charming little basket that she had woven of the green willows and decorated with moss and watercress. In the basket, on the cool, damp moss, and lightly covered with the cress, lay a half dozen fine rainbow trout.

"How pretty!" he exclaimed. "So that is what you have been doing!"

"They are for you," she said simply.

"For me?" he cried.

She nodded brightly; "For you and Mr. Lagrange. I know you like them because you said you were fishing when you heard my violin. And I thought that you wouldn't want to leave your picture, to fish for yourself, so I took them for you."

The artist concealed his embarrassment with difficulty; and, while expressing his thanks and appreciation in rather formal words, studied her face keenly. But she had tendered her gift with a spontaneous naturalness, an unaffected kindliness, and an innocent disregard of conventionalities, that would have disarmed a man with much less native gentleness than Aaron King.

Leaving the basket of trout in his hand, she turned, and swung the empty creel over her shoulder. Then, putting on her hat, she picked up her rod.

"Oh—are you going?" he said.

"You have finished your work for to-day," she answered

"But let me go with you, a little way."

She shook her head. "No, I don't want you."

"But you will come again?"

"Perhaps—if you won't stop work—but I can't promise—you see I never know what I am going to do up here in the mountains," she answered whimsically. "I might go to the top of old 'Berdo' in the morning; or I might be here, waiting for you, when you come to paint."

He was putting his things in the box—thinking he would persuade her to let him accompany her a little way; if she saw that he really would paint no more. When he bent over the box, she was speaking. "I hope you will," he answered.

There was no reply.

He straightened up and looked around.

She was gone.

For some time, he stood searching the glade with his eyes, carefully; listening to catch a sound—a puzzled, baffled look upon his face. Taking his things, at last, he started up the little path. But before he reached the old gate, a low laugh caused him to whirl quickly about.

There she stood, beside the spring—a teasing smile on her face. Before he could command himself, she danced a step or two, with an elfish air, and slipped away through the green willow wall. Another merry laugh came back to him and then—the silence of the little glade, and the sound of the distant waters.

With the basket of fish in his hand, Aaron King went slowly to camp; where, when Conrad Lagrange saw what the artist carried so carefully, explanations were in order.

Chapter XVIII

Sibyl Andrés and the Butterflies

On the following day, the artist was putting away his things, at the close of the afternoon's work, when the girl appeared.

The long, slanting bars of sunshine and the deepening shadows marked the lateness of the hour. As he bent over his paint-box, the man was thinking with regret that she would not come—that, perhaps, she would never come. And at the thought that he might not see her again, an odd fear gripped his heart. His thoughts were interrupted by a low, musical laugh; and he sprang to his feet, to search the glade with careful eyes.

"Come out," he cried, as though adjuring an invisible spirit. "I know you are here; come out."

With another laugh, she stepped from behind the trunk of one of the largest trees, within a few feet of where he stood. As she went toward him, she carried in her outstretched hands a graceful basket, woven of sycamore leaves and ferns, and filled with the ripest sweetest blackberries. She did not speak as she held out her offering; but the man, looking into her laughing eyes, fancied that there was a meaning and a purpose in the gift that did not appear upon the surface of her simple action.

Expressing his pleasure, as he received the dainty basket, he could not refrain from adding, "But why do you bring me things?"

She answered with that wayward, mocking humor that so often seized her; "Because I like to. I told you that I always do what I like—up here in the mountains."

"I hope you always will," he returned, "if your likes are all as delicious as this one."

With the manner of a child playfully making a mystery yet anxious to have the secret discussed, she said, "I have one more gift to bring you, yet."

"I knew you meant something by your presents," he cried. "It isn't just because you want me to have the things you bring."

"Oh, yes it is," she retorted, laughing mischievously at his triumphant and expectant tone. "If I didn't want you to have the things I bring—why—I wouldn't bring them, would I?"

"But that isn't all," he insisted. "Tell me—why do you say you have one more gift to bring?"

She shook her head with a delightful air of mystery "Not until I come again. When I come again, I will tell you."

"And you will come to-morrow?"

She laughed teasingly at his eagerness. "How can I tell?" she answered. "I do not know, myself, what I will do to-morrow—when I am up here in the mountains—when the canyon gates are shut and the world is left outside." Even as she spoke, her mood changed and the last words were uttered wistfully, as a captive spirit—that, by nature wild and free, was permitted, for a brief time only, to go beyond its prison walls—might have spoken.

The artist—puzzled by her flash-like change of moods, and by her manner as she spoke of the world beyond the canyon gates—had no words to reply. As he stood there,—in that little glade where the light fell as in a quiet cathedral and the air trembled with the deep organ-tones of the distant waters—holding in his hands the basket of leaves and ferns with its wild fruit, and looking at the beautiful girl who had brought her offering with the naturalness of a child of the mountains and the air of a woodland spirit,—he again felt that the world he had always known was very far away.

The girl, too, was silent—as though, by some subtle power, she knew his thoughts and did not wish to interrupt.

So still were they, that a wild bird—darting through the screen of alder boughs—stopped to swing on a limb above their heads, with a burst of wild-wood melody. In the arroyo beyond the willow wall, a quail called his evening call, and was answered by his mate from the top of the bank under the mistletoe oak. A pair of gray squirrels crept down the gray trunks of the trees and slipped around the granite boulder to drink at the spring; then scampered away again—half in frolic, half in fright—as they caught sight of the man and the maid. As the squirrels disappeared, the girl laughed—a low laugh of fellowship with the creatures of the wilderness—in complete understanding of their humor. Then—as though following the path of a sunbeam—two gorgeously brown and yellow winged butterflies came flitting through the draperies of virgin's-bower, and floated in zigzag flight about the glade—now high among the alder boughs; now low over the tops of the roses and berry-bushes; down to the fragrant mint at the water's edge; and up again to the tops of the willows, as if to leave the glade; but only to return again to the vines that covered the bank, and to the flowers that, here and there, starred the grassy sward.

"Oh!"—cried the girl impulsively, as the beautiful winged creatures disappeared at last,—"if people could only be like that! It's so hard to be yourself in the world. Everybody, there, seems trying to be something they are not. No one dares to be just themselves. Everything, up here, is so right—so true— so just what it is—and down there, everything tries so hard to be just what it is not. The world even sees so crooked that it can't believe when a thing is just what it is."

While watching the butterflies, she had turned away from the artist and, in following their flight with her eyes, had taken a few light steps that brought her into the open, grassy center of the glade. With her face upturned to the opening in the foliage through which the butterflies had disappeared, she had spoken as if thinking aloud, rather than as addressing her companion.

Before the artist could reply, the beautiful creatures came floating back as they had gone. With a low exclamation of delight, the girl watched them as they circled, now, above her head, in their aerial waltz among the sunbeams and leafy boughs. Then the man, watching, saw her—unheeding his presence— stretch her arms upward. For a moment she stood, lightly poised, and then, with her wide, shining eyes fixed upon those gorgeously winged spirits whirling in the fragrant air, with her lips parted in smiling delight, she danced upon the smooth turf of the glade—every step and movement in perfect harmony with the spirit of care-free abandonment that marked the movements of the butterflies that danced above her head. Unmindful of the watching man, as her dainty companions themselves,—forgetful of his presence,—she yielded to the impulse to express her emotions in free, rhythmic movement.

Instinctively, Aaron King was silent—standing motionless, as if he feared to startle her into flight.

Suddenly, as the girl danced—her eyes always upon her winged companions—the insects floated above the artist's head, and she became conscious of his presence. Her cheeks flushed and, laughing low,—as she danced, lightly as a spirit,—she impulsively stretched out her arms to him, in merry invitation—as though challenging him to join her.

The gesture was as spontaneous and as innocent, in its freedom, as had been her offering of the gifts from mountain stream and bush. But the man—lured into forgetfulness of everything save the wild loveliness of the scene—started toward her. At his movement, a look of bewildered fear came into her face; but—too startled to control her movements on the instant, and as though impelled by some hidden power—she moved toward him—blindly, unconsciously—her eyes wide with that look of questioning fright. He had almost reached her when, as though by an effort of her will, she stopped and stood still—gazing into his face—trembling in every limb. Then, with a low cry, she sank down in a frightened, cowering, pleading attitude, and buried her crimson face in her hands.

As though some unseen hand checked him, the man halted, and the girl's cheeks were not more crimson than his own.

A moment he stood, then a step brought him to her side. Putting out his hand, he touched her upon the shoulder, and was about to speak. But at his touch, with another cry, she sprang to her feet and, whirling with the flash-like quickness of a wild thing, vanished into the undergrowth that walled in the glade.

With a startled exclamation, the man tried to follow calling to her, reassuring her, begging her to come back. But there was no answer to his words; nor did he catch a glimpse of her; though once or twice he thought he heard her in swift flight up the canyon.

All the way to the place where he had first seen her, he followed; but at the cedar thicket he stopped. For a long time, he stood there; while the twilight failed and the night came. Slowly,—in the soft darkness with bowed head, as one humbled and ashamed,—he went back down the canyon to the little glade, and to the camp.

Chapter XIX

The Three Gifts and Their Meanings

The next day, Aaron King—too distracted to paint—idled all the afternoon in the glade. But the girl did not come. When it was dark, he returned to camp; telling himself that she would never come again; that his rude yielding to the lure of her wild beauty had rightly broken forever the charm of their intimacy— and he cursed himself—as many a man has cursed—for that momentary lack of self-control.

But the following afternoon, as the artist worked,—bent upon quickly finishing his picture of the place that seemed now to reproach him with its sweet atmosphere of sacred purity,—he heard, as he had heard that first day, the low music of her voice blending with the music of the mountain stream. Scarce daring to move, he sat as though absorbed in his work—listening with all his heart, for some sound of her approach, other than the melody of her song that grew more and more distinct. At last, he knew that she was standing just the other side of the willows, beyond the little spring. He felt her hidden eyes upon him, but dared not look that way—feeling sure that if he betrayed himself in too eager haste she would vanish. Bending forward toward his canvas, he made show of giving close attention to his work and waited.

For some minutes, she remained concealed; singing low, as though to try him with temptation. Then, all at once,—as the painter, with poised brush, glanced from his canvas to the scene,—she stood in full view beside the spring; her graceful, brown-clad figure framed by the willow's green. Her arms were filled with wild flowers that she had gathered from the mountainside—from nook and glade and glen.

"If you will not seek me, there is no use to hide," she called, still holding her place on the other side of the spring, and regarding him seriously; and the man felt under her words, and saw in her wide, blue eyes a troubled question.

"I sought you all the way to your home," he said, gently, "but you would not let me come near."

"I was frightened," she returned, not lowering her eyes but regarding him steadily with that questioning appeal.

"I am sorry,"—he said,—"won't you forgive me? I will never frighten you so again. I did not mean to do it."

"Why," she answered, "I have to forgive myself as well as you. You see, I frightened myself quite as much as you frightened me. I can't feel that you were really to blame—any more than I. I have tried, but I can't—so I came back. Only, I—I must never dance for you again, must I?"

The man could not answer.

As though fully reassured, and quite satisfied to take his answer for granted, she sprang over the tiny stream at her feet, and came to him across the glade, holding out arms full of blossoms. "See," she said with a smile, "I have brought you the last one of the three gifts." Gracefully, she knelt and placed the flowers on the ground, beside his box of colors.

Deeply moved by her honesty and by her simple trust in him; and charmed by the air of quiet, natural dignity with which she spoke of her gifts; the artist tried to thank her.

"And now," he added, "the meaning—tell me the meaning of your gifts. You promised—you remember—that you would read the pretty riddle, when you came again."

She laughed merrily. "And haven't you guessed the meaning?" she said in her teasing mood.

"How could I?" he retorted. "I was not schooled in your mountains, you know. Your world up here is still a strange world to me."

Still smiling with the pleasure of her fancy, she replied, "But didn't you ask me again and again to help you to know the mountains as I know them?"

"Yes," he said, "but you would not promise."

"I did better than promise"—she returned—"I brought you, from the mountains themselves, their three greatest gifts."

He shook his head, with the air of a backward schoolboy—"Won't you read the lesson?"

"If you will work while I talk, I will," she answered—amused by the hopelessness of his manner and tone.

Obediently, he took up his brushes, and turned toward his picture.

Removing her hat, she seated herself on the ground, where she had woven the willow basket for the fish.

After a moment's silence, she began—timidly, at first, then with increasing confidence as she found words to express her charming fancy. "First, you must know, that in all the wild life of the mountains there is no creature so strong—in proportion to its size and weight, I mean—as the trout that lives in the mountain streams. Its home is in the icy torrents that are fed by the snows of the highest peaks and canyons. It lives, literally, in the innermost heart and life of the hills. It seeks its food at the foot of the falls, where the water boils in fierce fury; where the current swirls and leaps among the boulders; and where the stream rushes with all its might down the rocky channels. With its muscles, fine as tempered steel, it forces its way against the strength of the stream—conquering even the fifty-foot downward pour of a cataract. Its strength is a silent strength. It has no voice other than the voice of its own beautiful self. And all its gleaming colors you may see, in the morning and in the evening, tinting the mighty heads and shoulders and sides of the hills themselves. And so, the first gift that I brought you— fresh from the mountain's heart—was the gift of the mountain's strength.

"The second gift was gathered from bushes that were never planted by the hand of man. They grow as free and untamed as the rains that water them, and the earth that feeds them, and the sunshine that sweetens hem. In them is the flavor of mountain mists, and low hung clouds, and shining dew; the odor of moist leaf-mould, and unimpoverished soil; the pleasant tang of the sunshine; and the softer sweetness of the shady nooks where they grow. In the second gift, I brought you the purity, and the flavor of the mountains."

"And to-day"—she finished simply—"to-day I have brought you the beauty of the hills."

"You have brought me more than the strength and purity and beauty of the mountains," exclaimed the painter. "You have brought me their mystery."

She looked at him questioningly.

"In your own beautiful self," he continued sincerely "you have brought me the mystery of these hills. You are wonderful! I have never known any one like you."

She was wholly unconscious of the compliment—if indeed, he meant it as such. "I suppose I must be different," she returned with just a touch, of sadness in her voice. "You see I have never been taught like other girls. I know nothing at all of the world where you live—except what Myra has told me." Then, as if to change the subject, she asked shyly, "Would you care for my music to-day?"

He assented eagerly—thinking she meant to sing. But, rising, she crossed the glade, and disappeared behind the willows—returning, a moment later, with her violin.

In answer to his exclamation of pleased surprise, she said smiling, "I brought my violin because I thought, if you would let me play, the music would perhaps help us both to forget what—what happened when I danced."

Standing by the gray boulder, with her face up turned to the mountains, she placed the instrument under her chin and drew the bow softly across the strings.

For an hour or more she played. Then, as Czar trotted sedately into the glade, she lowered her instrument and, with a smile, called merrily to Conrad Lagrange who, attracted by the music, was standing at the gate on the bank—from the artist's position invisible; "Come down, good genie,—come